PAST RECKONING

By June Thomson

PAST RECKONING

JUNE THOMSON

A CRIME CLUB BOOK

DOUBLEDAY

New York   London   Toronto   Sydney   Auckland

A CRIME CLUB BOOK
PUBLISHED BY DOUBLEDAY
a division of Bantam Doubleday Dell Publishing Group, Inc.
666 Fifth Avenue, New York, New York 10103

DOUBLEDAY and the portrayal of a man
with a gun are trademarks of Doubleday,
a division of Bantam Doubleday Dell
Publishing Group, Inc.

Library of Congress Cataloging-in-Publication Data
Thomson, June.
Past reckoning / June Thomson. — 1st ed. in the United States of
America.
p. cm.
"A Crime Club book."
I. Title.
PR6070.H679P37   1990
823'.914—dc20   90-33462
CIP
ISBN 0-385-41470-6
Copyright © 1990 by June Thomson
All Rights Reserved
Printed in the United States of America
October 1990
First Edition in the United States of America
RRD-H

CHAPTER ONE

It was easy enough to miss the museum. Nina Gifford came across it only by chance.

She had set out from the King's Head Hotel in Selhaven, fully intending to catch the 9:55 train into Chelmsford. From there she could get a bus to Althorpe, the village where she and Max used to live.

The trip was in the nature of a pilgrimage. Max might be dead but the house would still be there. She imagined it just the same as when Max had been alive, with the cedar tree on the lawn outside his bedroom window, the one he always said used to talk to itself in its sleep; his canvases piled up against the walls in the dining-room; even the summer-house where he used sometimes to paint and where he had died. Except she didn't really think of him as dead, only a very long way away. And that was the trouble. In London, it was difficult to get close to him; there were too many distractions. By going back to the house, she hoped she would be able to find him again. If Max was anywhere, it was there.

To begin with, all the omens for the trip had been good. The chain of hotels which owned the King's Head had advertised cheap three-day autumn breaks. In fact, it was seeing the advert in one of the Sunday papers which had first given Nina the idea. Selhaven wasn't far from Althorpe. Years ago, before Max's arthritis made it difficult for him to get about, they had quite often gone to Selhaven on the bus. The journey should be easy.

And then Danny—her brother with whom she shared a flat in Swiss Cottage—was going to be away in Birmingham for a week, staying with friends, so she wouldn't have to worry about cook-

ing for him, although the reason for his absence worried her.
God knows who the friends were or what he'd get up to. He'd
recently lost his job—chucked it, or so he said. Nina suspected
he'd been given the push.

Lastly, the weather was superb, one of those golden Octobers
—a real Indian summer. Seeing the sunlight falling on roofs and
chimneys and splintering off the windscreens of cars, Nina had a
sudden longing for the countryside, especially that rural Essex
landscape which Max had loved so much.

It was only after her arrival in Selhaven the previous afternoon
that the problems had begun to arise. Having made inquiries of
the hotel receptionist, Nina had discovered that the direct bus
from Selhaven to Althorpe no longer ran. It had been scrapped
several years before as unprofitable. The only way now to get to
the village was by train into Chelmsford, and from there by the
local bus, which ran only every hour. But whoever had drawn up
the timetables seemed to have taken a mischievous delight in
arranging them so that the most of the trains arrived ten minutes
after the Althorpe bus left. The only one that appeared to syn-
chronise was the 9:55 from Selhaven, the one which Nina had
intended catching as she left the King's Head.

Before setting out, she had taken pains to prepare herself for
the journey as carefully as if she really was going to meet Max at
the end of it. She had made a final check on her appearance in
the long mirror beside the reception desk as she crossed the hotel
foyer towards the swing doors, and had been pleased with the
image. It wasn't at all bad.

She was nearly fifty—no longer the schoolgirl who had fallen
in love with Max and run away with him. Her figure wasn't as
slim as it had been then, although her hair—even if it wasn't
quite the same rich red colour—was still striking enough to draw
the occasional appreciative male glance.

For Max's sake, she was wearing the new green blouse she had
treated herself to—terylene, although it looked and felt like real
silk—her good grey skirt, and because the weather was so warm,
just a short jacket of darker grey cloth. As a final touch, she had

put on her gold ear-rings, and black stockings because she had read in some women's magazine that they made your legs look thinner.

And then, when she was half-way down the High Street on her way to the station, the sun went in as suddenly as if someone had switched it off, and it began to rain—not a fine drizzle which she might have put up with, but a heavy squall which sent the drops bouncing back off the pavements and emptied the High Street of shoppers within seconds.

Seeking shelter in the doorway of Boot's, Nina peered out at the downpour. It was no good going back to the hotel for a raincoat and umbrella. In her optimism that the fine weather would continue, she had packed neither. There was nothing she could do except wait, hoping that the storm would soon blow over.

It eased eventually, but too late for her to catch the train. From the round-faced clock hanging in the window of the post office opposite, Nina could see that the time was 9:50, and the station was a good ten minutes' walk away. She'd never make it.

Sod!

The trip which had started out under such good auspices was already beginning to slide out of kilter, as if the focus of her luck had shifted.

Which was silly, she told herself. She could always make the journey the following day. Better to postpone it than kick her heels on the Chelmsford bus station for nearly an hour.

There remained the problem of what to do for the rest of the morning. The town centre was small and offered little in the way of diversion apart from the shops, the flint and stone church, All Hallows, and one or two nice old pubs. There was the river, of course, but she didn't want to go there quite yet. And it was too early for coffee.

There was no point either in hanging about in the doorway of Boot's, and, as the street began to fill up again, Nina set off in the direction of the church, taking the turning which ran beside it. Her intention was to walk round by the back roads and emerge into the main shopping centre further down, by which time she could decently find a café.

The road, Church Crescent, began ordinarily enough. It was lined with narrow, brick houses, each one with three steps up to the front door. In the overcast light, they looked mean, standing shoulder to shoulder, huddled under their wet slate roofs. But beyond them, the pavements widened out and the terraced cottages fell back to be replaced by larger, detached villas standing in their own gardens. There were even trees planted at regular intervals along the sides of the road in between the lampposts.

Nina walked slowly, stopping to admire some of the gardens, in which a few late-flowering roses still bloomed or a bed of yellow dahlias lingered where the frost had not yet cut them back.

At first sight, there was nothing about the museum to draw anyone's attention. It was, in fact, less attractive than several other houses in the street—a square, early Victorian building, rather prim and formal, with a flat facade of dark brick and long sash windows. An iron gate set into a high laurel hedge led into a front garden which was mostly lawn and neglected shrubbery, so that the house seemed to be buried in wet foliage. Fixed to the gate was a black-painted board on which was written in amateurish lettering the words: "The William Kershaw Museum. Open 9:30 to 4:30. Entrance 50p."

Nina nearly walked on past it. It hardly looked the place where one could spend a pleasant half an hour. She imagined it full of bits of old pottery and gloomy oil paintings. But in the absence of anywhere else to go to pass the time, Nina pushed open the gate and crunched up the gravelled path to the front door, where another hand-painted notice advised her to ring and enter.

Having done so, Nina found herself in a narrow entrance hall, papered in a leafy design which gave the impression that the garden had invaded the house. Straight ahead of her, an oak staircase went up to a shadowy landing. Several doors led off the hall, the one to her left set half-open, the one on her right closed and bearing another sign which announced "Strictly Private. No Admittance." Immediately inside the front door stood a small table on which were displayed a visitors' book, an old-fashioned black japanned cash box, together with a telephone and a rack of postcards, tenpence each, showing reproductions of a pen and ink drawing of the house, the perspective slightly awry. A tall brass cylinder, containing walking-sticks and with a pair of men's leather gloves laid across the rim, had been placed inconveniently near the door. Nina had to edge past it to get inside the hall.

The whole place smelt old and reminded her of Althorpe House—that same combination of forgotten dust, slightly peppery but not unpleasant, overlaid with the musty, church-like odour of damp plaster.

The house was also strangely silent, despite the sound of a woman's voice coming through the open door on Nina's left. The voice was saying in a brisk, matter-of-fact tone, "I hear another visitor has just arrived. Will you excuse me for a moment? In the meantime, do look round for yourself."

The next moment, the woman came out into the hall. She was tiny, in her sixties, with greying hair cropped very short, and a look of dark intensity about her, especially in the eyes, which Nina rather liked. There was, too, an odd mixture of practicality and eccentricity in her appearance, which seemed of piece with the house itself. She was wearing a sensible black dress, too long in the skirt to be fashionable, its drabness relieved by a great rope of amber beads which hung down to her waist, accompanied by a more utilitarian pair of spectacles on a cord. A man's watch was strapped to her wrist, and when Nina followed her to the table to pay her 50p entrance fee, which was placed in the cash box, she noticed the woman had little black velvet slippers on her feet, embroidered with Chinese peonies in pink and gold thread.

She thought how Max would have loved to paint her, especially that small, neat head, set at its alert angle, and the rich, golden-brown glow in the amber beads.

The woman was saying, in the same factual manner in which she addressed the other unseen visitor, "Before I show you round, I should explain that the museum is dedicated to the memory of my brother, William Herbert Kershaw, the poet and novelist who lived here from 1948 until his death seven years ago. I am, by the way, Imogen Kershaw. And now, if you'll follow me, we'll begin the tour. If you have any questions about my brother's life or work, please ask." Pushing open the door on the left, she gestured to Nina to precede her, adding, "This is the drawing-room, virtually unchanged since my brother's lifetime."

Going ahead of her, Nina was at first less aware of the room than of its occupant. He was a short, plump, middle-aged man in a grey suit, who was standing, head cocked and hands clasped behind his back, looking with great intensity at a small picture which was hanging by the fireplace. As they entered, he turned rapidly round to face them and, coming forward, said eagerly, "Ah, Miss Kershaw! May I claim you for a moment? I wanted to ask you about your brother's first editions. I see you have a fine collection. Is it complete?"

Nodding to Nina to excuse her, Imogen Kershaw moved away to the far end of the room where a huge glass-fronted mahogany bookcase occupied almost an entire wall, leaving Nina alone for a few moments to look about at her surroundings.

It was a double drawing-room, divided in the centre by folding doors which had been opened back to make one large area. The first half, in which Nina was standing and which overlooked the front garden, was furnished as a sitting-room. A pair of armchairs with wicker backs and loose cushions covered in faded cretonne were grouped round the fireplace, while an oval drop-leaf table was placed under the window. The rest of the space was taken up by a long, glass-topped cabinet which stood in the centre of the room.

Left to herself, Nina wandered over to it, peering down dutifully at its contents which were laid out as museum exhibits, each carefully labelled with a little typewritten slip of paper.

Like Miss Kershaw's man's watch and Chinese slippers, it was a bizarre collection of William Kershaw's personal possessions. His Brownie box camera and a small silver snuff box were placed next to his penknife and several pre-historic flint tools, picked up evidently, according to the label, by William Kershaw himself during his walks in the locality.

She wondered who William Kershaw was, never having heard of him, although her ignorance didn't surprise her. Max had often teased her about her lack of knowledge.

There were plenty of photographs of William Kershaw about the room, some standing on the shelves of an ugly overmantel while a particularly large reproduction hung immediately above it, hand-tinted to give the impression of an oil-painting. Nina went across the room to look up at it, and was disconcerted to find herself out-stared by very piercing dark eyes set in a long, bearded face. There was an expression of self-confidence about the set of the mouth which she didn't much care for. He looked as if he might want to gobble her up.

The framed snapshots on the shelves below were less intimidating. Here was William Kershaw in a Norfolk jacket and plus-fours standing in front of the house, holding a bicycle by the handlebars or, younger still and looking quite jolly in shirt-sleeves, pitchforking hay into a wagon. Those of him as a child seemed especially poignant. Such a self-possessed little boy who was now dead and buried! And, Nina mourned, I didn't even know he'd been alive.

William Kershaw's sister and the other visitor were still busy at the far end of the room, where Imogen Kershaw had unlocked the bookcase and was handing out some of the volumes for the plump man to examine.

Nina heard her say, "The book plate was designed by William himself. The owl was his own personal emblem. Suitable, don't you think?"

"Oh, highly," the plump man murmured in reply. "Athena, goddess of wisdom and patroness herself of the arts. . . ."

"And the rural connotations as well, of course," Miss Kershaw continued, her voice warming to the subject. "There used to be an owl which roosted sometimes in the garden. William could hear it calling as he worked here at his desk by the French windows."

Seeing they were absorbed in their conversation, Nina took the opportunity to glance quickly at the small picture hanging by the side of the fireplace which the plump man had been examining with such obvious interest when she had first entered the room.

It was a sketch in pencil and sepia wash of a woodland scene. In the foreground, a tree leaned at an angle, its trunk dense with shadows, the leaves strongly hatched in to convey the rich fullness of summer foliage. Beyond, the eye was led through more massed branches, as through an archway, to an oval of pure white in the background, suggesting a cloudless sky bleached by the summer heat. This brightness was echoed in a glint of water at the base of the tree where a stream or pool reflected the dazzle of sunlight.

The picture was badly framed, the white cardboard mount discoloured by age, and it appeared to be unsigned. But neither this omission nor the meanness of its narrow black frame could detract from the beauty of the drawing, nor dissuade Nina of its artistic merit. It was exquisite. And while she might know nothing at all about William Kershaw, she had learned enough from her years with Max to recognise the work of Samuel Palmer when she saw it.

Startled at finding this gem in such an unlikely setting, she turned quickly about, very much as the plump man had done, at the sound of Miss Kershaw's voice summoning her to the other end of the room where, it seemed, the tour was about to be resumed.

The rear section of the double drawing-room was devoted to Kershaw's literary life and had originally been his study, Miss Kershaw explained, although, when he had been alive, the folding doors had been kept closed to give him the privacy he needed.

Like the hall and the sitting-room area, the study was papered in a leafy pattern, the colours darkened by time so that it seemed, like the Palmer drawing, to be washed over with a sepia tint. But there any comparison ended. The general impression was of heaviness and gloom, unrelieved by the view through the French windows of the back garden, enclosed by a high brick wall, where a fine rain had begun falling again on more wet laurel leaves.

Nina began to fidget. She longed to go but it was clear that she would not be allowed to escape until the tour was over and she had examined William's swivel chair and desk, set at right angles to the window and laid out as it had been during his lifetime, with his Parker fountain pen, his notebooks and blotter. In the middle of the room, between the desk and the bookcase, stood another display cabinet, containing literary mementoes, including, as Miss Kershaw pointed out, several letters from such eminent writers as Bernard Shaw and Somerset Maugham.

Nina looked obediently about her, gazing with apparent interest at the books, at yellowing reviews pasted onto card and at more photographs of William. These included a studio portrait of him in academic cap and gown and one, framed in silver which stood on the desk, of William in a punt with friends, a young fair-haired man, exceedingly good-looking, in charge of the pole. From time to time, she also took surreptitious sideways peeks at the plump man, wondering who he was and what his interest in the Samuel Palmer drawing might imply.

He didn't look particularly artistic. The expensive quality about the cut of his suit and what was left of his grey hair— which was skilfully layered and puffed out to make the most of it —suggested a successful businessman.

He could be a dealer, Nina supposed, and instantly took a dislike to him for that reason, remembering Max's battles in the past with dealers and gallery-owners over what he considered their rapacity in making money out of other men's talents. There was one in particular, the last with whom Max had dealt and whom Nina could not bear to recall—not even his name.

Hurriedly, she transferred her attention to Miss Kershaw, who had moved towards the door leading into the hall, and who was announcing in her brisk, firm voice, "If you'd care to follow me upstairs, I'll show you William's bedroom and the manuscript collection."

She gave them no choice except to follow her, the plump man standing to one side to let Nina leave the room first and giving her, as she passed him, a look of sudden appreciation, as if up to that moment he had been too absorbed with the museum and its contents to notice her.

Nina was unsure of whether to be glad or sorry at such admiration. On the one hand, it was flattering that any man, even this one, should find her attractive. On the other, she mistrusted his intentions. To feel his eyes on her wasn't much better than being touched up by a stranger on a bus. As she followed Miss Kershaw up the stairs, Nina was acutely conscious of his presence immediately behind her and, when the three of them crowded into William's bedroom, she took care to remain just inside the door, out of reach of his eyes.

The bedroom was much of a muchness with the rooms downstairs. There was William's bed, a large single one with oak head- and footboards and a dark blue candlewick cover, very severe and masculine; William's chest of drawers with his silver-backed brushes laid out for inspection; even William's spectacles lying together with a book for bedtime reading on the side table.

As if, Nina thought with a shudder, the ghost of William himself might come up the stairs at any minute and, climbing into the bed, put on the spectacles, open the book where the strip of ribbon marked the page, and continue reading the poems of Rupert Brooke at the point where, in life, his literary studies had been suddenly cut short.

The image was so powerful that Nina hardly heard what Miss Kershaw was saying in answer to a question from the plump man —something to do with William's earlier career as a schoolmaster before becoming a writer.

"In Highgate, just before the war," Miss Kershaw concluded crisply.

She was standing at the bottom of the bed, one hand on the footboard as she spoke. It seemed to Nina that, for all Miss Kershaw's matter-of-factness, the gesture was oddly possessive, as if she were laying claim to William, asleep or awake, alive or dead. Nina found it disturbing. She saw in it a shadow of her relationship with her own brother, Danny.

From William's bedroom, they trooped along the landing, past more closed doors, to what Miss Kershaw called the manuscript room, Nina bringing up the rear. She wanted not only to distance herself from the plump man, but also from Miss Kershaw and the thoughts she had evoked about Danny. And not just Danny. There was Max as well. It suddenly occurred to Nina that, in planning to return to Althorpe, she was being almost as obsessive as Miss Kershaw in trying to cling to the past, which should be over and done with.

But what else have I left? Nina thought.

She hardly registered the manuscript room apart from a vague impression of walls lined with shelves filled with box files and large, buff-coloured folders, each one, like the items on display downstairs, carefully labelled. A desk was placed under the window, with a large, old-fashioned typewriter standing on it.

To Nina's relief, they returned downstairs shortly afterwards, Miss Kershaw again leading the way and announcing over her shoulder, for the benefit of both of them, "You'll sign the visitors' book before you leave? I like to keep a record of everyone who visits the museum."

Nina lingered in the hall, letting the plump man sign first. She pretended to look at some framed pages from one of William's notebooks hanging on the wall, containing spiky handwriting and several inept little sketches of landscapes and rural scenes, as she waited for him to go. She had the feeling that, should they leave the house together, he might offer to escort her.

He went at last and Nina moved forward towards the table to add her signature below his, glancing with curiosity at his name and address. He was, she discovered, Mr. Porlock, of Coleridge Avenue, London SW6. In the space left for comments on the far side of the page he had written, "An extremely interesting and valuable collection."

Valuable? The word seemed incongruous to Nina unless you included the Samuel Palmer drawing, which would fetch quite a tidy sum if it ever came up for auction, although to her, as it would have been to Max, its artistic worth far outweighed any financial consideration.

As she hesitated, wondering what comment to add, she noticed that the dates alongside the other signatures on the page covered a wide time span, going back to the beginning of the year. It would seem that the William Kershaw museum attracted few visitors.

The realisation prompted her to write a less than honest summary of her feelings—"Well worth a visit." Rather like, she thought guiltily as she laid down the pen, the sort of comment a teacher might make in an end-of-term report on a pupil about whom it was impossible to summon up a more positive response.

As a sop, she bought one of the postcards of the house—a reproduction of one of William's sketches, as she had suspected. Judging by the film of dust over its shiny surface, it had stood there on the rack unsold for many months.

"And do take one of these," Miss Kershaw added magnanimously, handing Nina her change and the postcard. She had taken from the drawer a single sheet of yellow paper, photocopied from a typewritten original, which it contained, Nina gathered, glancing at it quickly as she folded it and put it away in her handbag, a brief account of William Kershaw's literary life and achievements. "I can see how much you appreciated my brother's drawings. He often sketched when he was out walking. He said it gave him inspiration when he came to describe the same scene later in words. I think you'll agree he had some artistic skill, even if it was untrained?"

"Yes, indeed," Nina agreed, complying more with the second half of Miss Kershaw's remark than the first. Even so, it was

difficult to lie convincingly to Imogen Kershaw, who was standing very upright behind the table, fixing on Nina that direct,
dark gaze which put Nina in mind of her brother William's
portrait hanging in the museum.

Awkwardly, she turned to leave, in her haste colliding with the
brass cylinder full of walking-sticks which stood by the front
door, sending it tipping back against the wall. Miss Kershaw
came darting round from behind the table to help Nina set the
vase to rights, stooping to retrieve the pair of gloves which had
fallen to the floor and restoring them to their place on its rim.

It was a ridiculous and embarrassing situation.

Her colour high, Nina apologised and backed towards the
front door, feeling clumsy and graceless, a reaction in no way
helped when, on getting the door open, she found herself face to
face with a tall, good-looking, grey-haired man who was standing
on the step and seemed vaguely familiar.

"Sorry," Nina said again, edging past him, although why she
should apologise to him she had no idea.

The words were lost anyway in Miss Kershaw's greeting.

"Clive!" she was exclaiming with obvious delight. "I didn't
think I'd see you today."

"I'm afraid I can't stop long, Imogen," he replied. "I've only
dropped by on my way to the station."

Walking away from the house through the fine rain, Nina
wondered where she had seen him before—and so recently, too.
It was a small, niggling query, but one she preferred to concen-
trate on, rather than the embarrassment of her departure.

She was absurdly pleased when she was finally able to place
him. Of course! He was the tall, fair-haired young man in the
silver-framed photograph on William Kershaw's desk, the one
who had been holding the punt-pole—extremely good-looking,
which was why Nina had taken such particular notice of him. He
was much younger then, not more than nineteen or twenty. All
the same, it was still possible to recognise in Miss Kershaw's
visitor, Clive, the same smile, the same boyish look about the
eyes and forehead.

Satisfied at having made the connection, Nina turned out of the gate, thrusting to the back of her mind a vague feeling that she had left something behind in the museum, quite what she wasn't sure. She had taken only her handbag with her, and that was still hanging on her arm.

She could attribute the sense of loss to nothing more than that feeling of nostalgia for the past, which Miss Kershaw and the museum had aroused in her.

Perhaps it hadn't been such a good idea to come to Selhaven after all.

CHAPTER TWO

Nina spent what was left of the morning having coffee and looking round the shops, choosing an umbrella and then trying on
shoes which she had no intention of buying. Coming out of the
shoe-shop, she realised it had stopped raining and the sun had
come out, gilding the weathervane on All Hallows church.

It was now almost half-past twelve, too late to attempt the trip
to Althorpe, and she returned to her hotel bedroom to change
out of her damp jacket and tidy herself up before going downstairs for lunch.

It was while she was sitting in front of the dressing-table mirror, re-doing her hair, that she realised one of her ear-rings was
missing. Its absence accounted for that sense of loss which she
had felt on leaving the museum, for it was almost certainly there
where she had dropped it, during that damned stupid accident
with the brass walking-stick container.

The ear-rings, a pair of gold, pear-shaped drops, had been
given to her by Max for her birthday two years before his death,
the loss of one of them grieved her, although she consoled herself with the thought that she could easily return to the museum
to make inquiries. Besides, it would give her something to do
later that afternoon, which would have to be filled up somehow.

And tomorrow, she told herself, she'd go to Althorpe. After
all, she'd come all this way specially from London and she wasn't
going to be put off. To hell with Miss Kershaw and her museum.

Her mind made up, Nina went downstairs, feeling more
cheerful.

She liked the King's Head Hotel. It was comfortable but un-
pretentious, and smelt pleasantly of woodsmoke from the log

fires which had been lit in all the public rooms—even in the bar where, to celebrate her decision and the fact that the sun was out again, Nina treated herself to a gin and tonic before going into the dining-room.

Having lunched, she set off once more for the museum, sauntering along slowly and making the most of the afternoon.

Everything was transfigured by the sunlight, which had the rich, full quality of autumn—the colour of ripe yellow apples. The leaves of the sycamore trees lay pasted flat all along the pavements in Church Crescent, and filled the gutters in heaps like gold coins.

Even the museum looked transformed. The laurels in the front garden glistened with light while the tiny stones in the gravelled path, still damp from the rain, winked back at her as she walked towards the front door.

It was set open this time, allowing her a glimpse of the hall, the table with the visitors' book still displayed although the cash box had gone. The door on the right, the one marked "Strictly Private," was also ajar.

It was from there that the sound of voices came, merely conversational as Nina approached along the path, but raised in sudden anger as she reached the porch.

She heard Miss Kershaw's first, the crisp tone no longer matter-of-fact but with a decided edge to it.

"I don't think it's any of your business, Ambrose."

And then a man's voice, much less in control.

"I simply don't want to see you making a fool of yourself."

"A fool!" Miss Kershaw's voice grew sharper. "I would have thought that you of all people, one of William's oldest friends . . ."

The man broke in.

"It's that damned girl who's given you the idea."

"Lucy had nothing whatever to do with it," Miss Kershaw retorted. "I make up my own mind although I admit her appreciation of William's work helped me come to a decision. As a matter of fact, she's calling round here later this afternoon."

"Oh, Imogen, for God's sake!"

The man's voice rose in exasperation.

Nina backed away, retreating on to the lawn where her footsteps would be inaudible, and walking quickly towards the iron gate which she shut quietly behind her.

Shielded by the laurel hedge, she stood for a moment in thought. It was clearly not the time to inquire about her missing ear-ring. She would have to come back later when Miss Kershaw's visitor had left. An hour should be long enough. In the meantime, she would have to find something else to do, she supposed. Walking back to the town centre, she turned this time away from the King's Head towards the river, taking the long route round in order to spin out the time.

She had not wanted to visit it quite yet. Her plan had been to see Althorpe House first, find Max there, or whatever remained of him—ghost, spirit, some lingering essence of his personality, even she wasn't quite sure—and then, although she hadn't rationalised this either, she would walk with him along the river bank, past the boats at anchor and the sliding water, past the Barge pub and the row of fishermen's cottages, and say to him, "Look, Max! Do you remember it? Nothing's changed."

But she feared it had. And she was right.

In the years since she and Max had last visited it, the place had altered almost beyond recognition.

The approach to it was still the same, past an area of open ground round which the road swung in a great arc before disappearing off into the flat Essex landscape towards the distant coast. But what had once been rough grass, set with a few benches and a couple of rusty swings, was now neatly landscaped with ornamental shrubs and trees. There was even a pair of public lavatories, discreetly tucked away inside their own shrubbery. The wooden hut with the let-down counter, which had once served tea and thick cheese sandwiches, had been replaced by a proper snack-bar, all glass and white-painted concrete, with a little paved terrace in front where plastic tables and chairs were stacked up, the season being over.

The river was still there, of course, the brown water running low in the channel, leaving the boats, drawn up along the bank, lying tilted at anchor in the mud, their masts jostling against the low sky-line. The mud itself still glistened with the same oozy richness, and the sea-gulls swooped and hovered as she remembered them doing when she and Max had last walked there, shrieking as if pinned to the wind, their legs streaming out behind them.

As for the Barge, where Max had sat on the steps to sketch the view across the marshes, it was so changed that she couldn't at first believe it was the same pub. With its brickwork colour-washed pale pink and blue shutters added to the windows, it looked like a sentimental illustration from a children's fairy-tale, some god-awful cottage in the woods made out of sugar and gingerbread.

The cottages, too, had been tarted up with brass carriage lamps and fake bow windows.

God, how Max would have hated it! Nina thought, and felt some of his anger touch her.

Not even the old boat-building shed which stood at the far side of the cottages had been spared. Stripped of its creosoted clapboarding, the spaces in the frame had been filled with lumpy white plaster, the beams themselves painted black to give it a Tudor appearance. The big double doors, through which had come the sound of hammering and the sweet smell of sawdust, had been replaced by a shop facade above which hung a sign announcing "Harbour Antiques" in Gothic lettering.

Nina went up to peer in at the window, drawn despite herself by a seascape displayed on an easel, along with a cabinet of blue and white porcelain and a boule chest.

The painting was good; a little too self-consciously Turner-esque perhaps, in the clouds and flying spray and lacking, now she was close up to it, that feeling of air and water dissolving together which Max had taught her to admire when he had taken her to the Tate to see the real Turners.

As she stood examining it, she was aware of the interior of the shop beyond the top of the frame, richly lit by lamps which glowed on polished wood and silver and on the figures of two men, who were deep in conversation as they moved towards the door. As the light fell across their faces, she saw one of them was plump with grey hair.

Turning on her heel, Nina hurried away. She had no wish to encounter Mr. Porlock again, although, remembering his interest that morning in the Samuel Palmer drawing at the museum, his presence in the antique shop struck her as ominous.

She wondered if she ought to say something to Miss Kershaw about him; warn her perhaps. But of what? Mr. Porlock could be entirely innocent of any ulterior motive, being merely, as Nina herself was, a visitor to the town who happened to admire beautiful things whether they were antiques or art.

The museum, when she returned to it, seemed normal. The front door was now closed and the house—as Nina paused on the step, listening attentively before knocking—was silent.

Miss Kershaw herself, opening the door, appeared calm and composed, inviting Nina inside the hall and regarding her with a bright, interested gaze as Nina explained the purpose of her visit.

Yes, the ear-ring had been found, Miss Kershaw assured her, adding, "Mrs. Gifford, isn't it? I looked up your name and address in the visitors' book in case I had to post it back to you. I've put it away safely. Do come in."

Opening the door on the right, she ushered Nina into a room which overlooked the front garden. Although it was furnished in the same style as the rest of the house, and contained more mementoes of William Kershaw in the way of photographs set out along the mantelpiece, it was more a private sitting-room than part of the museum. The display cabinets were absent, and in their place were chintz-covered armchairs, reading lamps and ornaments, while the chimney alcoves were filled with shelves containing books other than Kershaw's.

A low table was standing in front of the fireplace, covered with a linen cloth and set with two cups and a tea-set in flowered china, together with a plate of digestive biscuits. Evidently a guest was expected for tea, almost certainly the girl referred to in the quarrel which Nina had overheard, and whom Miss Kershaw had spoken of as Lucy.

This knowledge, learned through eavesdropping on the doorstep, made her feel guilty and, when she had thanked Miss Kershaw, who had retrieved the ear-ring from a small china dish on the mantelpiece, she felt obliged to add, "I very much enjoyed looking round the museum this morning."

Because it wasn't true, the remark came out in a quick little rush of words, but Miss Kershaw seemed gratified. Smiling, she gestured to Nina to sit down in one of the armchairs.

"I'm so glad you like it. We don't get many visitors, I'm afraid."

The candour of Miss Kershaw's last comment almost disarmed Nina into not noticing her use of the word "we." It could have referred collectively to Miss Kershaw and the museum, or could have been merely a conversational ploy on Miss Kershaw's part to avoid speaking directly of herself. But Nina was as disconcerted by it as she had been by the sight of Miss Kershaw's hand resting on the foot of her brother's bed and felt, as she had then, that William Kershaw still inhabited the house. Indeed, for an absurd moment, she wondered if the second teacup placed in readiness on the table was not for some mortal visitor after all, but had been put there for William's use.

She was further discomposed by Miss Kershaw's next remark.

"Have you read any of my brother's books?"

She was leaning forward in her chair, so that the long rope of amber beads swung down into her lap, her black dress starkly decorative against the flowered fabric, and her head set at a quizzical angle as she waited for Nina's reply.

Nina said brightly, "I'm afraid I haven't. But I will. I suppose I could order them from the library."

"Yes, you'll have to," Miss Kershaw replied in her practical manner. "They're all out of print now, I'm sorry to say. But I'm quite sure you'll enjoy them. William had this very special gift

for describing the rural background. Do you like the countryside?"

"Oh, yes, very much," Nina agreed.

That, at least, was true.

"And you're visiting the area?"

"Yes, just for a few days."

Nina almost added that she had lived for several years in Althorpe but had the sense to keep her mouth shut. The village
was only ten miles away from Selhaven. Miss Kershaw might
make the connection between the name Gifford and the circumstances of Max's death, which had featured on the front pages of
all the local newspapers.

To turn the conversation away from herself, Nina continued,
"It's a very attractive house."

"Yes, isn't it?" Miss Kershaw replied. "William fell in love
with it as soon as he saw it. Of course, it takes a lot of upkeep.
These older houses do, don't they?"

The remark prompted Nina to wonder how Miss Kershaw
managed. She had the impression that money was short. The
house certainly had a shabby air about it, although some of that
was the result of preserving the rooms exactly as they had been
in William Kershaw's lifetime. Even so, looking about her, Nina
noticed details of the room which suggested the place was run on
a tight budget. The red turkey carpet on the floor was almost
threadbare in places, the white linen tablecloth carefully darned.

Nina recognised the signs and sympathised. At Althorpe
House, she'd had the same struggle to make ends meet.

She said, picking up one of Miss Kershaw's earlier remarks,
"So it isn't the family home? I thought you might have lived
here as a child."

Miss Kershaw looked amused.

"I can see you haven't read the little pamphlet I gave you this
morning," she replied. "In it, I've set out a brief resumé of
William's life. You'll also find a list of his books. So, if you want
to order them from the library you'll know what titles to ask for,
won't you?"

Aware that she'd put her foot in it again, Nina felt the colour rise in her face. The pamphlet was lying forgotten in her handbag among a jumble of other pieces of paper, together with the phone number in Birmingham where Danny could be reached and which she had insisted he give her just in case. But in case of what, she wasn't sure.

"An emergency," she had replied when he had insisted on pinning her down to an explanation.

"Like what?"

"Well, in case I'm taken ill."

It was unlikely. She was as strong as a horse. But her persistence had worn him down and, with bad grace, he had scrawled a number on the back of an old envelope which he chucked across the table at her.

The memory of it struck a jarring note in Miss Kershaw's sitting-room, especially when Nina could see only a few feet away from her photographs of another brother displayed with such obvious pride and affection.

Nina gathered up her handbag in readiness to go.

As she did so, there was a ring on the front doorbell and Miss Kershaw, getting to her feet to answer it and aware of Nina's intention to leave, said, "Do stay and meet Lucy."

Nina sank back in her chair, curious to meet the girl referred to in the quarrel she had heard taking place earlier in that very room.

The girl, Nina saw when Miss Kershaw ushered her in, was young, attractive and intelligent-looking. Perhaps as a compliment to Miss Kershaw, she was dressed, like her, entirely in black, in a plain jumper and a full, softly gathered skirt, her thick dark-blond hair, the colour of honey, tied back with a large, black petersham bow at the nape of her neck. The visual impression was simple and yet at the same time fashionably Continental, like, Nina thought, a left-bank student or a young Parisian businesswoman. When Miss Kershaw introduced her to Nina as Lucy Blake, the young woman's expression, alert and self-assured, and the manner in which she extended her hand, bore out Nina's impression.

And yet, like the seascape in the antique shop window, although all the elements were there, they didn't add up satisfactorily.

Under the young woman's apparently attentive manner, Nina sensed an irreverence, almost an arrogance, which could have been nothing more than the self-confidence of youth. Miss Kershaw seemed unaware of it. The introductions over, she and Lucy Blake were discussing one of William's books which Lucy Blake had just returned and which she had evidently borrowed the previous week.

She was saying, "I enjoyed it so much, Miss Kershaw. I thought the descriptions were even better than in 'Winter's Discontent.' And the ending was superbly handled."

Miss Kershaw smiled, bending her head in acknowledgement of the tribute before getting up to replace the volume in the alcove bookshelves. When her back was turned, Lucy Blake exchanged a glance with Nina as if seeking her approbation as well.

See how superbly I handle *her*, that glance seemed to be saying.

It made Nina feel uncomfortable. She had no wish to be drawn into any conspiracy, however subtle, with Lucy Blake. Besides, she wasn't quite sure what the game was or indeed if any game were being played. She only knew that, since the young woman's arrival, the focus of attention in the room had shifted away from Miss Kershaw to the girl, seated so gracefully by the window, the autumn sunlight itself seeming to conspire to shine directly through the glass on to the mass of her fair hair.

Miss Kershaw appeared not to have noticed the change of emphasis which had taken place in her own sitting-room. In her usual brisk, practical manner, she was saying, "I'll put the kettle on. Won't you stay and join us for tea, Mrs. Gifford?" as if she were still in charge of the situation.

But Nina had made up her mind.

"Thank you but I really must go," she said, and managed to

make her exit with more dignity on this occasion, merely nodding to Lucy Blake before saying goodbye to Miss Kershaw, who had accompanied her to the front door.

"And thank you again for finding the ear-ring," she added.

"Not at all," Miss Kershaw assured her. "Do call in again any time."

"Yes, I certainly will," Nina said, lying agreeably, with no intention of doing anything of the sort.

She had had quite enough of the William Kershaw museum.

At the gate, glad to be finished with the place, she took a last look back at the house, so prim and formal among its surrounding leaves, as if none of the little cross currents of emotions and tensions that Nina had witnessed had touched its outward appearance at all.

CHAPTER THREE

About an hour later, the tea-party over, Lucy Blake also left the museum, bending down to kiss Imogen Kershaw's cheek and carrying away with her another of William's novels, *The Idyll,* carefully wrapped in a clear plastic bag.

As Nina had done a little earlier that afternoon, Lucy turned left at the end of Church Crescent towards the river, although her destination was not the marina itself, nor the picturesque cottages which clustered near it.

East Lane ran behind the Barge public house, a narrow side-street of small terrace houses, not yet gentrified although a few had come up in the world and boasted hanging baskets and new white paint. Number fourteen was not one of these. A battered green van, its bonnet raised, stood outside the front door, which was also set open, giving a view of a cramped passage and a staircase which rose precipitously, like a set of steps ascending a cliff. The sound of Heavy Metal music coming from the front room behind closed curtains was almost visible, too, as if the notes were hammering at the air itself and pounding the late afternoon sunshine into atoms.

Lucy let herself in and, stalking across to the record player, switched it off and flung open the curtains in two such abrupt movements that silence and light seemed to erupt simultaneously. In the sudden brightness, the room and its occupant were revealed, both looking startled and dishevelled, Jed scrambling up from the sofa, the furniture appearing to leap into focus in the same guilty manner.

It was second-hand stuff, its shabbiness emphasised by the litter of other objects strewn about—magazines, discarded clothes, dirty plates and cups. A bunch of dusty sea-lavender was stuffed into a small, flower-patterned jug on the mantelpiece, while a car battery, attached to a charger, stood on a sheet of newspaper next to the hearth.

Jed looked as tousled as the room itself. Dressed in jeans and a leather jerkin—which might have been bought at the same back-street dealer's as the furniture—he was tall and powerfully built, with heavy features and thick, dark hair, the sides shaved close to the head, the back left long and twisted into a short queue like a sailor's pigtail. Bare arms bulged out of the sleeveless jerkin, the right forearm tattooed with an eagle, the left with a half-open rosebud—as incongruous as the piece of china on the mantelpiece.

"So how was the old bag?" Jed asked.

"All right," Lucy replied indifferently. She went over to the fireplace to put the novel Miss Kershaw had given her down on the mantelshelf, next to a tobacco tin and a packet of cigarette papers.

"Got another book, I see," Jed remarked. "For Christ sake, Luce, what's the point you keep going round to see her? I mean, you've never got nothin' out of it except for that bit of old china and bloody books."

"But I do," Lucy corrected him coolly. "More than you realise. And you're not to touch it. I don't want your oily great thumb-prints all over the cover. I've got to return it next week." Taking off the petersham ribbon, she shook out her hair so that it sprang loose about her shoulders before assuming a pose, one elbow on the mantelshelf, the other hand clasped dramatically to her forehead as if in deep thought. "What shall I say about this one when I see her? Something about the narrative drive, I think. 'He carries one along with such enormous energy, like a river at high tide.' "

Jed grinned admiringly up at her.

"Christ, you're a bloody case, Luce. And talking about rivers, you haven't forgotten it's Wednesday? With a bit of luck, we might get a pick-up date tonight."

"The boat's all right?" Lucy asked, suddenly alert.

"Yeah, yeah," he assured her. "I checked the engine this afternoon while you was out. Goes like a dream. And I've got the van's battery on charge for the run out to the Bells." He nodded across to where it was standing on its sheet of newspaper. "It's all sorted."

He got up from the sofa and came over to her, putting his arms round her and pulling her close so that he could smell her hair.

"Feel like it?" he asked, and ran one hand down to her breast.

"Why not?" she said and, pushing his hand away, went across the room to shut the curtains as abruptly as she had opened them.

Nina treated herself to tea in the same café where earlier that morning she had had coffee.

Afterwards, wondering what to do with the rest of the afternoon, she went to look round All Hallows, where a lady in a hand-knitted twin set sold her a booklet about the church. Nina put it into her handbag with the stuff from the Kershaw museum before walking away to look at the de Boisville Crusader monument, which the lady assured her was particularly fine.

The de Boisvilles, husband and wife, lay on top of their tomb, their hands joined meticulously together, finger to finger, the way children pray. He was in his Crusader armour, sword at his side and a lion at his feet, she in a long sculptured robe, a little dog at hers, their heads resting on tasselled stone cushions.

Despite their uncomfortable resting place, they looked at ease, Nina thought. She imagined them in life, sharing a double bed but in more intimate contact, the husband, divested of his armour, turned on one side, his arm across the woman's shoulders, while she lay curled up against his hip, the way she and Max had always slept.

Like a fool, Nina felt tears come suddenly to her eyes, although it was years since she'd wept for Max. Sniffing them angrily away, she moved on, deliberately turning her attention to the east window, the brasses in the floor, the sixteenth century font and the nineteenth century pulpit, until the light began to fade and the lady in the twin set started to put away the booklets and the postcards and the printed notice which read: "Make Your Own Brass-Rubbing. Inquire At Desk For Details."

Outside, it had grown dusk—and quite cold, too. There seemed to be nothing else to do except go back to the hotel, where Nina had another bath, her second that day, before changing and going down for dinner.

Returning to her room, she checked the bus and train timetables for the following day, assuring herself that the 9:55 from Selhaven really did connect with the bus for Althorpe with the minimum delay. As for coming back, she was inclined to leave that to chance rather than attempt to work out the Continental 24-hour system, which seemed to operate after midday.

She wondered if, while she was at Althorpe, she should call on Lionel who, she imagined, was still living in the village. He'd hardly have moved away; he was a creature of habit. But she decided against it. Reviving the past would only embarrass him. Besides, what on earth would they say to one another?

Before returning the timetables to her handbag, she resolved to give it a damn good clear-out of its accumulated rubbish. Out it all came tumbling onto the bed—the keys to the flat; her purse and cheque-book; her comb, which could do with a wash; her compact, spilling a little powder onto the hotel's bedcover as it rolled free; and finally, the booklet from All Hallows church. Wedged infuriatingly at the bottom were the pamphlet and postcard from the Kershaw museum which, once she had released them, set free a small cascade of loose change and old receipts from the supermarket, together with the torn envelope on which Danny had written down his phone number in Birmingham.

There was a telephone on the bedside table.

I could ring him, Nina thought. It wouldn't really be checking up on him. I could simply say I'll be back on Friday, and will he be home by the weekend so that I'll know what shopping to get?

But the number, once the receptionist had given her an outside line, rang and rang unanswered, until Nina finally replaced the receiver with an odd feeling of foreboding.

Although he could be anywhere, Nina told herself. Having a drink with those friends of his. Or out for a meal.

But she hadn't the heart to do much after that, and stuffed most of its contents back inside the bag with the exception of the Kershaw pamphlet and postcard, both of which, after a cursory glance, she tore up and dumped in the waste-paper basket, remembering, as she did so, that she had said nothing after all to Miss Kershaw about Mr. Porlock, the other visitor to the museum.

Well, it was too late now. She wasn't going to go back there.

That done, she got ready for bed, propping herself up on the pillows to watch the late-night film on the television set, which stood on its own little shelf on the far side of the room, and trying to persuade herself that the trip was going to be a success and worth every penny it would cost her.

Ambrose Scott also tried unsuccessfully to make a telephone call that evening, in his case to Imogen Kershaw.

On first returning home after their quarrel, he had been inclined to let the matter rest. Imogen was stubborn, especially where anything to do with William was concerned, but she was no fool and eventually she would come round to his point of view.

Far better to let it all die down.

But, as the evening wore on, he grew more guilty and restless. He was an habitual worrier; even he admitted this. Anxiety was stamped all over him, from the long-nosed, mournful face to the ungainly body which seemed ill at ease inside his own clothes. When he hoisted his tall frame out of the chair to cross the room to the telephone on his desk, even the room seemed too small to accommodate him comfortably.

He had an awkward, perching walk, like a heron, diffident and oddly-angled, with a similar questing, forward thrust to the head and shoulders.

His initial call at half-past eight was unanswered, for which Ambrose was grateful and not over-concerned. Imogen could be having a bath or working upstairs in the manuscript room. In the latter case, if she heard the phone, she was more than likely to ignore it, having adopted William's attitude to outside distractions when he was absorbed in some more interesting activity than chatting to friends.

He'd try ringing her again later, Ambrose decided. The delay would give him time to think out what he wanted to say to her, for he had dialled her number with no clear idea of how he would patch up their quarrel.

He'd have to apologise. That much was certain. Imogen would never climb down first. In that respect, she had grown increasingly like her brother, as if, after his death, she had acquired more and more of William's quirks of character.

Years before, when she was still in her teens and Ambrose had first fallen in love with her, she had been very much William's younger sister, any eccentricities of behaviour lying dormant and so overshadowed by her brother's more dominant personality that Ambrose had been unaware of them, seeing only a small, slim girl with fine, dark eyes and a direct manner. Capable, too; she had run that house in Highgate and looked after not only William and any friends he brought down from Cambridge, but her widowed father as well.

Not that Imogen had taken much notice of Ambrose, treating him, to his secret sorrow, as merely one of William's friends— "the tall one," as he had once heard her describe him with that objective matter-of-factness which had become more apparent as she grew older.

If she had any other softer feelings left over from her adoration of William, they had been for Clive, William's other Cambridge friend and also a regular visitor to the Highgate house. Clive, Ambrose supposed wryly, would have to be summed up in an Imogen-type phrase as "the good-looking one." Certainly, as a young man, Clive had been spectacularly handsome, like a youthful Rupert Brooke; lithe, blond and possessing that diffident charm which women tended to find irresistible.

Even so, it had been William who had dominated their trio—the planet round which Ambrose himself and Clive had revolved like satellite moons. As for Imogen, she had been William's constant star.

He tried calling her again at a quarter to ten, letting the phone ring for several minutes, but there was still no answer and this time he replaced the receiver with greater uncertainty.

Should he try again? Or should he leave it until the morning?

As a compromise, he rang Clive. God knows why, except that Imogen might have told Clive about her plan and it would be interesting to hear his reaction—useful, too, if Clive disapproved of it as strongly as he himself did. Between them, they might be able to talk her into changing her mind.

Ringing Clive would also have the benefit of assuaging his own guilt. If he couldn't apologise to Imogen, at least he could own up to someone about the quarrel.

But he had no better luck with Clive's number than with Imogen's.

Mrs. Wharton, Clive's housekeeper, answered the phone.

Mr. Osborne, she informed him, had gone to London for the day and wasn't home yet.

"Ask him to call me when he gets in," Ambrose said, and hung up.

He filled in the intervening time as best he could. Feeling too unsettled to read, he made himself coffee, which he normally didn't drink that late in the evening, as it tended to keep him awake. Carrying the cup back to the sitting-room, he folded himself down into the armchair, where he sat waiting for Clive to ring him.

The public-house, the Ring of Bells, on the outskirts of Chelmsford, was crowded. Jed had to use his shoulders to squeeze a space for himself and Luce at the bar where he could see the clock, tapping with a coin on the counter until the barman came over to serve him with a pint of lager and a vodka and tonic.

"Cheers, mate," Jed said, pocketing the change and turning his head to look round casually at the other customers. There was no-one he recognised.

"See anyone?" he asked Luce.

She shrugged indifferently.

"What does it matter who it is?" she asked.

"Yeah, I suppose you're right," he agreed.

He'd've liked to put a face to the man, though; give him an identity. He didn't have Luce's cool. None of it seemed to touch her, not the trips over to the Bells, nor the times they took the boat out to pick up the stuff. Not even when he screwed her. She was as far away then as she always was, on some bloody little island of her own where he couldn't reach her. It was him who got worked up.

Like now.

He could feel the tension beginning to churn in his stomach, so that when the clock hands pointed to a quarter to ten, he really did need a leak.

"Shan't be a tick," he told Luce and pushed his way across to the door marked "Toilets."

The passage beyond was empty; so, too, was the gents', apart from a man standing up having a pee at the far side who left as Jed entered. He was an elderly bloke in specs; not his contact, he thought, although there was no way of telling.

Jed shut himself up in the middle cubicle, bolting the door and seating himself on the lav while he waited and listened, but he could hear nothing except water running and the far-off sound of voices from the bar.

And then suddenly the voices sprang nearer as the door was opened. Footsteps crossed the tiled floor and someone entered the cubicle next to his.

Jed cleared his throat.

"That you, Doug?" he asked.

He could never make it sound natural; he always felt bloody stupid when he asked the question.

No answer as per usual, only the slip of paper pushed through the gap under the partition.

Jed picked it up and read the typewritten note before tearing it up, as he'd been instructed, and dropping the bits into the pan.

He pissed on top of them, watching as they sank and then were whirled away in the rush of water as he pulled the chain.

Returning to the bar, he joined Luce, who was being chatted up by some geezer in a suit and tie.

"Naff off, sunshine," Jed said pleasantly and grinned when the bloke moved away.

"All right?" she asked, meaning had he made contact?

"Yeah," he said. "You ready to go?"

They went out to the van.

A Merc was driving away from the car-park—Doug's perhaps. Who could tell? It wouldn't take a car like that more than half an hour to make it down from London on the motorway. He watched its rear-lights disappear with a pang of envy. It was all right for some—the big boys, them at the top.

"So?" Luce asked, getting into the passenger seat. "When's the collection?"

"Early Sunday morning," he told her. "One thirty; high tide. Pick up point's just beyond the estuary, off Deacon's Sand. Should be dead easy."

He made the last remark to convince himself that it really would be, and to try to control that tremble of fear and excitement which, like the urge for a screw, was beginning to creep up him in its own dark tide.

"Of course it will," Luce said.

Only she really meant it.

At ten thirty-five, less than an hour after Ambrose had rung his number, Clive Osborne passed through the barrier at Selhaven station and, having handed in his ticket and wished the

clerk goodnight, emerged onto the forecourt from where he set
off to walk home. He chose a more direct route than the one he
had taken that morning when he had called in briefly to see
Imogen.

Living within walking distance of the station, he rarely bothered to use the car, preferring the exercise—a habit he had kept
up since his undergraduate days when he regularly played tennis,
rowed or swam.

He still liked to keep in shape, and it was a source of secret
pride that his weight and measurements hadn't changed since he
was thirty.

Part of his reason for going to London was to see his tailor and
to get a decent haircut. There was no-one locally whom he could
trust. He sometimes wondered if he wouldn't be better off selling up and moving to London. Since he had retired, there was
nothing to keep him in Selhaven except that the place, like
everything else, had become a habit, and habits were difficult to
break.

He turned into Marchwood Avenue, feeling the air from the
river against his face, smelling of salt and mud and the recent
rain. He remembered with a sudden, startling clarity an occasion
years ago, just after the end of the war, when he and William
and Ambrose had walked along the river bank at Tolstead where
William was then living, William striding along with his head
flung back and shouting verses from "The Owl and the Pussy-
cat" into the wind.

Odd lines of it came into his mind as he walked up the drive
to the front door; God knows why.

> "They took some honey and plenty of money
>   Wrapped up in a five-pound note. . . ."

He found his key, but before putting it into the lock, he rang
the front doorbell to let his housekeeper, Mrs. Wharton, know
he was home. Since his wife's death, she had become nervous of
being left alone in the house after dark, which he could under-

stand. The place was some distance from its neighbours, standing in its own grounds.

She met him in the hall, her face full of relief at his return, as
if, he thought with momentary exasperation, she were the wife
and he the errant husband. All the same, he smiled as, putting
down his brief-case, he waited for her to make her usual comments.

"I'm so glad you're back, Mr. Osborne. Let me take your coat.
Supper's ready in the drawing-room."

The ham sandwiches would be placed on the drinks tray next
to the whisky decanter—one of those long-standing habits which
was so hard to break.

Taking off his coat, he started to say, "I'm sorry I'm later than
usual, Mrs. Wharton. I just missed the ten past eight
train . . . ," but she was running on with an unexpected, addi-
tional remark.

"And Mr. Scott phoned earlier this evening. He asked if you'd
ring him back as soon as you got in."

Clive felt suddenly exhausted.

Damn Ambrose! What on earth did he want that couldn't
keep until the morning?

Picking up the hall extension, he dialled the number as Mrs.
Wharton went up the stairs carrying his overcoat.

When the phone finally rang, Ambrose scrambled up out of
his chair so quickly that he nearly knocked over his coffee cup in
his eagerness to get to it.

"Ambrose? I gather you wanted me to ring you. What's it
about?" Clive asked. His voice sounded tired and oddly distant,
as if the request had come at an inconvenient time.

Hearing it, Ambrose began to regret his earlier anxiety. He
was probably making a great deal of fuss about nothing. But it
was too late now to retract. He'd have to offer some explanation.

All the same, he felt foolish as he plunged into his account,
speaking quickly in order to get it over and done with in the
shortest possible time.

"It's about Imogen. I'm afraid I had rather a row with her this afternoon. The point is, Clive, I've tried phoning her a couple of times this evening and there's no reply. I wondered if she was all right. You didn't happen to see her today at any time?"

There was a small silence in which he felt he could hear Clive's surprise at his excuse for making the phone call, which even to Ambrose himself sounded absurdly lame.

Then Clive said, "I saw her only briefly this morning on my way to the station. I've been in London all day. As a matter of fact, I've only just got in. She seemed perfectly all right then. When did you see her?"

"This afternoon," Ambrose admitted.

"Then you spoke to her after I did. Was she ill or anything when you saw her? I don't quite understand why you're so concerned."

Put that way, Ambrose himself could find no rational cause for his anxiety, apart from his own guilt. He was aware also that the conversation was beginning to slip beyond his control, leaving him feeling vulnerable and exposed, standing there alone with the telephone receiver to his ear.

"No, no," he said hurriedly. "She wasn't ill. Just rather angry." Then, in a little flurry of candour, he continued, "I feel rather awful about quarrelling with her, Clive. I mean, I've known Imogen for years. And so have you, of course. I realise she can be exasperating at times. But I wanted to apologise. And then, when she didn't answer the phone . . ."

His voice trailed away.

"What was the quarrel about?" Clive asked.

Ambrose seized gratefully on this change of subject.

"Well, that was really why I wanted to speak to you. I wondered if she'd mentioned it to you."

"Mentioned what?"

"This scheme of hers for trying to get William's books republished. . . ."

"Was that all?"

"All?" Ambrose asked, uncomprehending. "I should have thought it was more than enough."

Clive said, "I'm sorry, Ambrose. I didn't make myself very clear. I meant, did she talk about her other idea of paying to have at least some of them printed privately if she can't get a publisher interested?"

"Good God!" Astounded, Ambrose could think of nothing else to add.

Clive was saying, "Look, Ambrose, take my advice—just leave it for the time being. The whole thing's way over the top. To begin with, I don't think she's got any idea of the cost of private printing, quite apart from the problem of finding a publisher who'll want to take them."

"No, quite," Ambrose agreed, adding, in case the remark sounded disloyal to William's memory, "I mean, good though his novels are, fashions have moved on since his time. Pity, but there you are."

"Leave it," Clive repeated, more impatiently this time. "There's nothing much else you can do for the moment. Can we discuss it some other time? Frankly, I'm rather tired. It's been quite a heavy day."

"Of course, of course," Ambrose agreed. "Sorry, Clive."

But the apology went unheard. Clive had already hung up.

Ambrose replaced his own receiver humbly, and returned to his chair. All the same, despite Clive's advice, he felt he couldn't let the matter rest. The conversation, intended to assuage his own conscience, had left him more troubled than before. Nothing had been resolved; only more problems raised. And it hadn't settled his basic concern—which he still couldn't rationalise—about Imogen's refusal to answer the phone.

It was past eleven o'clock—too late to try ringing her again, in case she had gone to bed.

As for himself, sleep was out of the question. He felt wide-awake, his mind stimulated by Clive's remark, coming out of the blue like that, about Imogen's idea of paying for William's books to be published.

How in God's name did she intend financing it? The whole idea was crazy.

No, not crazy, he corrected himself. Crazy meant mad and Imogen wasn't that. But certainly eccentric. Obsessive also where William was concerned.

William himself had been decidedly eccentric in the last years of his life. And so had old Mr. Kershaw, the father. Ambrose remembered him from the Highgate days, just before the war, going on and on about spiritualism until Imogen had taken the situation in hand by briskly changing the subject.

Some of that remembered decisiveness of hers seemed to activate him.

He'd walk round to the house, he decided. He wouldn't sleep anyway, and the exercise would help to counter the effects of the coffee, another stimulant which added to his wakefulness.

It was a fine night, he saw when, having put on his overcoat, he let himself out of his front door. The sky had cleared after the heavy rain earlier in the evening and there was a breath of coming winter in the air.

The High Street was virtually deserted, apart from a group of youths and their girl-friends larking about outside the Wimpy bar.

To avoid them, Ambrose went on to the pedestrian crossing, where he paused scrupulously to make sure there was no traffic coming before walking over to the other side and turning down Church Crescent.

The street was empty, many of the houses already in darkness. So, too, was Imogen's.

He paused to look through the iron gate which closed off the front garden. No lights showed anywhere; not even in the hall nor in her bedroom, which faced the road.

All the same, he pushed open the gate and went a few yards inside, keeping to the lawn so that the sound of his footsteps on the gravel wouldn't disturb her and where he stood for several moments contemplating the facade before turning back, reassured.

She'd gone to bed, he told himself. So all that anxiety had been for nothing. As he'd thought earlier, she'd probably spent the evening going over William's manuscripts in readiness for approaching a publisher, and had chosen to ignore the phone.

He'd ring her in the morning, he thought. Turning back, he let himself out of the gate and began to walk quickly away, passing beneath a street-lamp a few yards further along the pavement.

As he did so, a uniformed constable, in top coat against the night cold, who was pacing slowly along on the far side of the road, paused and watched Ambrose's departure as he strode along awkwardly on his long legs and disappeared from sight in the opposite direction.

CHAPTER FOUR

Despite the walk to the museum and the reassurance it had given him, Ambrose slept badly, going over and over in his mind the quarrel with Imogen and rehearsing what he would say when he finally contacted her.

She even invaded his dreams. On waking, he couldn't exactly recollect them. All he could recall was a confused memory of standing with her in a room—not in the museum; it seemed to be the Highgate house, only it was so dark that he wasn't sure. William was there, too. Ambrose couldn't see him but was strongly aware of his presence, and heard his laughter. And then the dream seemed to shift inexplicably to a sea-shore. He was alone, walking along the beach and looking for William and Imogen, who had been with him but were now lost. He kept calling to them, he remembered, and thinking he heard their voices, but they were only the cries of sea-birds answering him.

He woke early with an overwhelming sense of loss which was absurd. But absurd or not, he jittered with impatience until he could telephone Imogen at the museum, which he did precisely at eight o'clock. Knowing a little about her routine, he was quite sure she would be up by then and having breakfast. She was an early riser and her mornings were taken up exclusively with domestic tasks, shopping or dusting and cleaning the house, including the museum, before opening it to the public. As far as he knew, she worked on William's papers or her own accounts only in the evenings.

The phone again rang unanswered.

He let it ring for nearly five minutes, imagining Imogen coming down the stairs or along the hall from the kitchen to pick up the receiver. But no-one came.

Finally, he replaced his own receiver and, his mind made up, put on his overcoat and left the house.

At first sight, the museum looked perfectly normal. The gate was shut, the garden undisturbed. It was only when he was half-way up the path that he realised anything was wrong.

All the curtains, including those of the museum and of Imogen's sitting-room to the right of the front door, were still drawn.

He rang the bell, keeping his finger on the button for several long seconds although he knew it wouldn't be answered.

Standing there on the porch, he tried to rationalise his feelings.

She could have overslept.

Unlikely, he told himself.

Then she could be ill.

It was a possibility.

But it was small consolation, and he forced himself to face the fear which he had already acknowledged in his dream.

Imogen had died like William, suddenly and without warning, snuffed out in her sleep as he had been. No goodbyes. No hint of impending dissolution. No word of farewell to friends.

He felt suddenly very angry. God damn her, it was so bloody selfish!

The rage released in him an urge for action.

There was a path which led round to the back of the house, rarely used and littered with fallen leaves. It was narrow, squeezed in between the building and the high laurel hedge which separated the garden from the one next door.

Ambrose ran clumsily down the path, knees and elbows jutting, and, rounding the corner of the one-storey addition which housed the kitchen and the scullery, came to a halt on the area of worn, moss-covered flagstones which surrounded the rear of the house.

Here two entrances faced him—the back door which led into

the kitchen, and the French windows which opened directly into the room, now part of the museum, which used to be William's study.

The back door was locked. Ambrose rattled the handle in vain. The French windows would also be locked, he assumed. He was contemplating smashing the kitchen window and climbing in over the sink when, turning away to find a stone with which to break the glass, he noticed the little chips of fresh wood which littered the paving-stones under the French windows—the curtains of which were still closed—and the long scar in the paintwork where the two leaves had been prised apart.

For some inexplicable reason, the panic and fear drained out of him, leaving him cold and empty. Quite calmly, he walked over to the windows and pushed with the flat of his hand against one of the leaves, which swung partly inwards, prevented from opening fully by William's desk which stood at right angles to it. Edging his way past it and dragging back the curtains as he went, Ambrose entered the room.

He was half-prepared for what he would find. Logic told him that the house had been broken into and that the motive was theft. Even so, he was brought to a sudden standstill by the sight of the room.

It was the silence which was so shocking. In it, the smashed cabinets seemed mute witnesses to a destructive force which had been voiceless as well as faceless, and which still brooded over the scene, so that for several seconds Ambrose himself stood dumb and motionless.

He forced himself forward, hearing his feet crunch on broken glass and a voice, which he assumed was his, shouting Imogen's name, although he did not recognise it and had no recollection of even opening his mouth.

She was lying in the sitting-room. He had to switch on the light in order to see her.

Afterwards, when the police questioned him, he was able to remember doing that, and to recall the reasoning behind his action. The room was dark because the curtains in there were also closed.

He also remembered how stiff and uncomfortable she had looked, although he had no clear memory of how she was lying, except there was blood all over her face. He knew without needing to touch her that she was dead.

Seeing her, the phrase "blood-boltered" came into his mind—God knows from where. *Macbeth,* wasn't it? He seemed to connect it with Banquo's murder. But he didn't mention that to the police.

Nor did he properly register William's walking-stick lying close to her body—the one with the heavy, silver knob—although he must have seen it, for he remembered thinking afterwards that it was William's favourite.

His next clear memory was of picking up the phone in the hall and dialling 999.

A voice, male and oddly reassuring, asked him to remain where he was.

"I'll wait outside," Ambrose said, and replacing the receiver very quietly in order not to disturb the silence, he let himself out by the front door into the garden, where he walked about on the lawn until the police car arrived.

In her hurry to get herself ready for the trip to Althorpe, Nina forgot the umbrella she had bought the day before, and had to return to her bedroom to collect it.

Coming down the stairs for the second time, she was aware of the atmosphere of suppressed shock and excitement which, in her brief absence, seemed to have overtaken the foyer. There was a small huddle of people round the reception desk, consisting of the receptionist herself, the head waiter and a young man in a business suit whom Nina had never seen before, and who took himself off as soon as Nina approached to hand in her room key.

"I'm sorry," the receptionist said, apologising presumably for whatever had been going on, which still seemed to distract her.

"Is something wrong?" Nina asked.

It was pure nosiness. She was on her way to the station, and after all, it was none of her business. But the receptionist, a young, local girl, friendly and inclined to chat, which Nina liked, had clearly not recovered from the shock of what had happened. Her eyes were still wide with an expression of disbelief.

She said quickly in explanation, "That was my boy-friend, Mrs. Gifford. He works next door in the bank. He just dropped in to tell me there's been a murder."

"Murder?" Nina repeated.

The word seemed to batter at her heart, knocking all the breath out of her.

Murder! She knew then that she couldn't go to Althorpe.

"He was on his way to work," the girl was continuing, "when he saw the police car. He lives practically opposite, you see, in one of the big houses which have been turned into flats; just round the corner from here, as a matter of fact. It can't be more than ten minutes' walk away. It's the museum—I don't suppose you'll have heard of it, hardly anybody has—but it seems someone broke into it last night and murdered the woman who runs it."

Suddenly aware of Nina's reaction, she broke off to ask anxiously, "Are you all right, Mrs. Gifford? I hope I haven't upset you. Perhaps I shouldn't have said anything."

"No, no," Nina assured her, finding her voice at last. "I think I've caught a chill. All of a sudden, I felt very cold."

She had indeed begun to shiver. The feeling of breathlessness had been replaced by an icy coldness which seemed to have settled in her hands and legs. She could feel her kneecaps and the back of her calves tremble with it.

The receptionist came out from behind the desk and, taking Nina by the arm, began to lead her towards the hotel lounge.

"I think you ought to sit down," she was saying. "I'll order tea for you."

She beckoned to the head waiter who was still hovering in the foyer before installing Nina in one of the armchairs.

Sitting very still and upright in the chair, her umbrella in her lap, Nina could see them behind the glass panes in the door, glancing in at her and whispering together. Then the head waiter went away and the receptionist resumed her place behind the desk, looking subdued and guilty.

The tea came, carried in by a waitress, with a strip of aspirin tablets lying on the tray beside the sugar bowl.

Carefully, Nina re-arranged herself, placing her umbrella and handbag on the empty chair beside her before leaning forward to pour herself tea.

At the same time and with equal deliberation, Nina put her thoughts into order as if they, like the milk jug and the teapot, needed to be handled with caution in case they spilt over.

She thought about Miss Kershaw first. It was impossible to imagine her dead. Instead, Nina concentrated on the living woman she had seen only the day before, tiny and brisk and upright in her old-fashioned black dress and Chinese slippers, going up the stairs or sitting, as Nina herself was doing, in front of a low table set for tea.

The memory reminded her of the young woman, Lucy Blake, and the quarrel Nina had overheard concerning her.

And then there was Mr. Porlock and the Samuel Palmer drawing.

Nina supposed she ought to contact the police but shrank from doing so. She'd have to give her name and perhaps explain what she was doing in Selhaven in the first place, and then everything would come out. She dreaded that happening, more for Max's sake than her own.

Which brought her to Max and the visit to Althorpe.

Bending forward, Nina picked up the strip of aspirins and, breaking open the foil covering, tipped two of the tablets into the palm of her hand where they lay very white and round.

She ought to take them, she thought. The receptionist must have ordered them specially, prompted no doubt by guilt over the part she had played in Nina's sudden indisposition. To spurn them would seem deliberately churlish and unforgiving as if Nina were indeed blaming the girl.

She swallowed them obediently with a little tea, feeling them dissolve with a bitter flavour at the back of her throat.

She couldn't go to Althorpe now, not just because it was too late to catch the train, but for a more cogent reason. How could she hope to find Max there after what had happened to Miss Kershaw? Even in her own mind, Nina couldn't form the word "murder." It was a form of betrayal.

People were beginning to come into the lounge—hotel residents and women shoppers looking for somewhere warm and comfortable to have coffee and meet their friends.

One of them came and stood by the chair opposite Nina, loosening her coat.

"Is this seat taken?" she asked.

"No," Nina said. "I'm just going anyway."

As the woman sat down and began arranging her own possessions round her, laying claim to the vacant space, Nina collected hers and got to her feet, wondering where she could go.

Not back to her bedroom. The thought of sitting up there alone was unbearable.

There seemed to be no other option except to leave the hotel.

And she would have to go to the police. Walking away across the lounge to the foyer, Nina came to that decision. In an odd way, she felt she owed it to Miss Kershaw and to Max, too, although she herself couldn't quite understand why. It was something to do with facing up to the truth as he had done, sitting out there alone in the summer-house at Althorpe.

But not quite yet. Like him, she felt she needed to sit down somewhere quietly by herself first, and think it all through.

The girl looked up as Nina passed the reception desk.

"Are you feeling better, Mrs. Gifford?" she asked.

"Oh, yes, much," Nina replied, smiling to give credence to the words. "And thank you for the tea."

Outside the hotel, she stood on the pavement uncertainly, jostled by the passers-by, as she wondered which direction to take. Then, catching sight of the tower of All Hallows church, she began to walk towards it.

She would have preferred to wait inside the church itself but, remembering the lady in the twin set who was in charge of the postcard-table and preferring solitude, Nina sat down on one of the wooden seats in the churchyard.

It was small, a mere triangle of ground with the church at its apex and the rest laid out with paving and grass in which a few worn head-stones leaned at angles. But there were narrow flower-beds lining the paths and even a couple of trees, a yew and one that Nina didn't recognise. Its leaves drifted slowly down off the branches as she sat there and watched. It was peaceful, too, despite the traffic which passed up and down the High Street less than twenty yards away behind the wall.

And warm. Sheltered by the wall and the bulk of All Hallows itself, the churchyard seemed to gather up all the sunlight as if in a great golden bowl.

Gratefully, Nina turned her face towards the sun, sitting so still that a squirrel ran across the grass and came to rest only a few feet away from her, upright on its haunches and feeding delicately from something it was holding between its front paws, which were like tiny hands.

And then the clock on All Hallows struck the hour, the squirrel darted away up the tree and Nina, feeling rested and quieter inside, rose to her feet.

It was time to go.

CHAPTER FIVE

Detective Chief Inspector Jack Rudd of Chelmsford CID stood just inside the door of the William Kershaw museum. He was listening, head cocked, to the local Inspector, Bayliss, who had arrived at the house before him, and who was giving him details of the discovery of the body. Behind him, Rudd's Detective Sergeant, Boyce, was taking notes.

As he listened to Bayliss, Rudd looked about him, taking rapid, surreptitious glances, first to his left where, through a half-open door, he could see what he assumed was the museum itself. A display cabinet, its glass cover smashed, stood just within his line of sight. To his right, through another open door, he could glimpse the scene of the murder where the Scene of Crime officers, in white coveralls and protective boots, were already at work.

It was a sitting-room, judging by its furniture.

Curtains drawn, he noted. Overhead light on but not the lamps.

From time to time, the room was more brilliantly illuminated by flash as McCullum, the police photographer, took shots of the scene.

Bayliss, thank God, had too much already on his own plate to want to linger over his report. Speaking in his own form of shorthand, he was saying, "Body was discovered at 8:20 this morning by a Mr. Ambrose Scott, friend of the dead woman. Gave a short report to the uniformed men in the patrol car who answered his emergency call. Rang from here, it seems." He indicated the telephone which stood on a small table near the front door. "Didn't have much to say to them. Too shocked.

He'd gone home by the time I got here. You'll want his address?" As Rudd nodded, Bayliss read it out from his own notebook. "Number twenty-four Liston Road, that's the turning on your right off the High Street just past the post office. I assume you'll want to interview him."

"Yes, but later," Rudd said. "I'd like to know first about the dead woman."

But beyond Bayliss's precise topographical directions, his information didn't seem to stretch that far.

"Name's Imogen Kershaw. Can't tell you much else about her except she'd been living here since just after the war. Evidently ran this place in memory of her brother William who died a few years back. A writer, it seems. Heard of him?" When Rudd shrugged, Bayliss said with a grin, "Neither have I. Got too many damned reports about real life to read without bothering with fiction. There's a pile waiting for me on my desk now." He was already stowing away his notebook in readiness to leave. "If you want me, you know where to find me." As a parting comment, he added, one foot over the threshold of the front door, "Looks to me like a burglary which went wrong. You'll find the French doors at the back have been forced open."

Even after Bayliss had gone, Rudd seemed in no hurry to take over the investigation. Hands in pockets in a characteristic pose, he remained standing in the hall, letting the house settle down after the Inspector's departure, his head to one side as if listening to the atmosphere.

He was a stocky, middle-aged man with the bland, open features of a countryman rather than a professional policeman—an appearance he took some pains to cultivate. It had its uses, especially when interviewing. On these occasions, he preferred to give the impression of the sympathetic copper, cocking an attentive ear, and leaving it to Boyce—his Sergeant, who was much better built for the part—to play the role of the heavy.

While Boyce waited, trying to control his impatience, Rudd contemplated his surroundings, but whatever the dark patterned wallpaper, the framed drawings or the table by the door with its visitors' book and rack of postcards had to say to him was evidently for his ears alone for, after a few minutes of silent musing, he jerked his head at Boyce and, using his elbow, shoved open the door which led into the museum and stepped inside the room.

The experts, still occupied with the scene of the murder, had not yet moved into this part of the house and the museum was empty apart from Rudd and his Sergeant, who followed the Chief Inspector as he strolled about, gazing round at its contents like any ordinary visitor.

The tinted photograph of William Kershaw came in for particular scrutiny. Rudd stood for several moments studying the bearded face and the half-smile which quirked up the corners of the mouth, then, skirting round the broken glass which lay on the floor by a shattered display cabinet, he moved into the rear part of the double-room, where he halted again. This time it was the French windows which claimed his attention, and the desk and chair which stood at right angles to them. But he said nothing, merely nodding as if satisfied with what he had seen, and then turned aside towards a large mahogany bookcase. He paused in front of it, with his head tilted to one side, while he read out loud some of the titles printed on the spines of the books behind the glass doors.

" 'Late Harvest,' 'The Judas Kiss,' 'Heron Reach.' Heard of any of them, Tom?"

But before Boyce could reply, he was off again, this time to the middle of the room to contemplate a second display cabinet. Its top had been prised open and some of its contents were missing, judging by the gaps between the remaining objects and the scattered typewritten labels, which still lay in place at the bottom of the case.

Some of these he also read out loud.

" 'William Kershaw's cigarette case.' 'William Kershaw's watch and chain, bequethed to him by his father, George Frederick Kershaw,' " adding, half to himself, "I wonder what else is missing? Perhaps there's an inventory somewhere. Or the man who found the body can give us a list. What's his name?"

"Scott," Boyce told him. "Ambrose Scott."

But Rudd appeared to have lost interest. He was looking towards the front part of the room which they had first entered, and where the other large cabinet was standing, its glass top shattered.

"Odd don't you think, Tom? Someone breaks in, presumably through the French windows over there," nodding towards them, "prises open one cabinet and yet smashes the other."

Boyce shrugged but said nothing. He knew the Chief Inspector in this mood. He would wander about, apparently aimlessly, commenting out loud on certain aspects of the scene of the crime, often those which seemed to the Sergeant the least relevant to the investigation.

"We'll get those photographed and printed," Rudd continued. "And these as well."

He had crossed back again to the French windows beside the desk, coming to a halt in front of the double leaves. He was less interested, it seemed, in the broken lock—and the bolts which had been forced away from the frame at the top and bottom of both doors—than in the curtains, roughly dragged to one side, and the distance between the left-hand leaf and the desk. Using his elbow again, he swung the door experimentally to and fro a couple of times, but he made no comment. Instead, he squatted down on the threshold to peer at the flakes of paint and the tiny slivers of wood lying on the paving-stones below the door before craning his neck round to look up at the lock itself.

"Flimsy," he remarked. "Wouldn't have taken much to break it open; nor the bolts, come to that. And whoever did it seems to have used something sharp. Come and have a look, Tom. A knife, was it? Or a screwdriver?"

He stood aside to let Boyce examine the lock and the gashes in the frame where the wood had been sliced into.

"Could be either," Boyce said.

But Rudd wasn't listening. He was looking past the Sergeant at the view of the garden.

It was a long, rectangular plot, mostly grass, apart from the paved area immediately behind the house and so thickly set along the boundaries with trees and bushes, many of them evergreens, that it was impossible to see much of the neighbouring houses, apart from the line of roofs and chimneys.

At the far end, the garden was bounded with a high brick wall, swagged with ivy, in the centre of which a heavy wooden door stood ajar.

"We'll take a look at that later," Rudd remarked. "Find out where it leads to."

"Don't you want to see the body?" Boyce asked.

"Not yet," Rudd said cheerfully.

He seemed in good spirits; God alone knew why. As far as the Sergeant could see, they had done nothing except wander about the museum, examining evidence of a break-in which, as Bayliss had pointed out, had gone badly wrong.

And it appeared the tour was not yet over for, returning to the hall, the Chief Inspector headed off down the passage towards the back of the house, opening doors as he went and revealing, in turn, a gloomy dining-room which overlooked a side-path, also lined with evergreens, which seemed little used; and a sunnier breakfast room at the far end of the passage.

"Looks as if Miss Kershaw usually had her meals in here," Rudd remarked, nodding towards a table laid with a gingham cloth and salt and pepper pots. "And the kitchen's through here," he continued, going down two steps. "Back door locked. And bolted, too. Scullery beyond," opening another door, "but no outside access apart from that tiny window. So what do you make of it, Tom?"

He had come to rest by a deep, old-fashioned sink, which occupied the space under the kitchen window beside the back door. He propped himself against it and indicated with one hand not just the kitchen itself but what lay beyond it, a gesture which seemed to encompass all that they had seen so far, from the broken lock and bolts on the French windows to the garden door left ajar.

"You're not convinced it was a break-in," Boyce said, chancing his luck. It was more of a statement than a question and was said in almost an accusatory tone of voice, as if he suspected the Chief Inspector of keeping something up his sleeve.

Unrepentant, Rudd grinned at him with the same good humour.

"Not entirely, Tom," he admitted, "although I'm prepared to keep an open mind. But by my book, it looks more like a break-*out* than a break-*in.*"

"I don't get you," Boyce said.

"All right then. Let's try to reconstruct our supposed burglar's movements. What do you think they were?"

Boyce began cautiously.

"Well, I suppose he came in through the back gate . . ."

"Could be," Rudd conceded. "Go on."

". . . forced open the French windows and started rifling the museum when Miss Kershaw . . ."

He was spared the task of completing the sentence by the arrival of Kyle, the young, fresh-faced Detective Constable, who tapped on the open kitchen door before announcing, "The pathologist's just arrived, sir."

"Right!" Rudd said, heaving himself away from the sink. "Let's go and have a look at the body and find out what Pardoe makes of it."

Pardoe, a short, sandy-haired man, was still in the act of wiping his feet vigorously on the doormat as Rudd and Boyce returned along the passage to the hall. Overcoat open, medical bag gripped in one hand, he seemed impatient to get down to business, an impression confirmed by his brusque greeting, "Morning!" followed immediately by the question, "Well, where is it?"

"In here," Rudd told him, pushing open the door to the left of the hall but remaining just inside the room, as Pardoe bustled forward to lay claim to the body.

Someone, presumably one of the SOCO's, had drawn the cur-

tains and the sunlight now flooded in, turning the electric light
from the overhead lamp pallid and revealing an interior of which
Rudd had so far caught only an oblique glimpse.

For the first few moments, he seemed content to look about
him, absorbing the details of the room rather than the body, as if
preferring first to place it in its setting. Later, he would examine
the video and McCullum's still photographs and remind himself
how it had looked, but for the time being, he was more interested in taking his own mental shots.

It was a pleasant, shabby room, furnished with the sort of
heavy, old-fashioned stuff which might have been bought at auction or inherited from parents. Rather too cluttered with objects
for Rudd's taste. Now that he was living alone—his widowed
sister who had kept house for him having left to re-marry—he
had made a clean sweep of any knick-knacks which collected
dust.

The mantelshelf was crowded with ornaments and photographs of William Kershaw. Even across the width of the room,
Rudd could recognise the bearded face which he had already
seen in the large, tinted portrait hanging in the museum.

Plenty of books, too, filling the alcove shelves; one was lying
on an occasional table, an envelope acting as a bookmark, pro-
truding from the pages. A lamp stood beside it, and from the
position of an armchair drawn up close to both table and lamp,
Rudd surmised that this was Miss Kershaw's customary seat.

And now to Miss Kershaw herself.

Her body was lying not far from the chair, in the space between it and the fireplace, fully clothed in a black dress and a
grey cardigan, a pair of spectacles hanging on a cord round her
neck and a man's watch on her wrist. These serviceable and
sensible objects contrasted with the more exotic details of her
appearance, including a long rope of amber beads and a pair of
embroidered silk slippers, one of which had fallen off, revealing a
foot clad in a lisle stocking.

She lay on her back, the right arm flung out, the left folded across her chest; her legs drawn up slightly and also turned to the right.

Quite tidy, Rudd noticed. Apart from the blood, that is, which covered her face, making it difficult to see her features. It had run down from several deep wounds on the front of the head, matting her grey hair and forming a dark stain on the carpet beside her.

A man's walking-stick, its heavy silver knob tarnished with blood, lay not far from the body. It was receiving particular attention from Wylie, who was kneeling beside it, painstakingly removing grey hairs from its surface with a pair of tweezers before placing them inside a small, clear, plastic envelope.

The murder weapon, evidently.

Even before Pardoe spoke, Rudd had already a damned good idea of what had happened in that room.

She had been struck as she lay on the floor. Although he was no medical expert, the Chief Inspector had seen enough head wounds in his time to recognise the results of downward blows. Besides, the body lay too neatly. Someone felled in a standing position would drop any old how, legs and arms splayed out.

From the neat way in which the body was lying, it looked to Rudd as if someone had tried to lift her up and then, giving up the attempt, had struck her several times on the head with the walking-stick.

In panic? he wondered. And what was she doing on the floor in the first place?

It was a question answered by Pardoe, who looked up from his examination to comment briskly, "Three blows to the forehead, one at least heavy enough to fracture the skull and cause haemorrhaging to the brain although I'll need to have her on the slab to confirm that. All struck from above and, in my opinion, while she was lying on the floor. One minor wound to the back of the head, not as severe as the others but sufficient to break the skin and possibly cause unconsciousness."

Wylie looked up from his task of picking hairs off the walking-stick to comment, "We found blood on the fender, sir. She could have hit her head on that."

Rudd took a few steps inside the room to get a better view of the fireplace. Its hearth was surrounded by a fender of the type he remembered from his own childhood home, the iron base topped off with a low guard of pierced brass, the edge of it sharp enough to cut open the head of anyone who fell heavily against it.

Pardoe was saying, "I'll carry out the PM later today. In the meantime, you can move the body when you want to. I've finished with it for now."

Rudd cocked an eyebrow at Wylie who nodded in agreement, meaning the body had been measured and photographed, its clothing taped. It was ready for bagging up before being placed in a coffin shell and taken away.

In the hall, Pardoe shrugged on his overcoat and marched off to his car, parked in the road outside.

Shortly afterwards, the body also left, wheeled on a trolley in its coffin along the gravel path and through the iron gate to the waiting hearse, where a crowd of neighbours had gathered on the pavement. They all had apparently just happened to leave their houses at that precise moment to go shopping or to walk their dogs, more interested in the dead Miss Kershaw than they had ever been in the living.

After the hearse's departure, Rudd seemed to move into a higher gear, sending McCullum to photograph the interior of the museum, with special instructions to take close-up shots of the French doors, while some of the uniformed men were despatched to search the gardens.

"Not you, Kyle," Rudd added, as the men moved off. "There's a visitors' book on the hall table. Make a note of the names and addresses of anyone who's signed in over the last three months. And I don't want your prints all over it, so use a pen or something to turn the pages."

He retreated again with Boyce to the breakfast-room, where

Kyle joined them within a few minutes, his notebook open at the page on which he had copied down the information.

"There's ten names, sir," he said, "going back to last April."

"Which suggests the place wasn't exactly doing a roaring trade," Boyce put in.

"Any recent ones?" Rudd asked.

"Two dated yesterday," Kyle told him.

"Yesterday!" Rudd perked up at once. "Who were they?"

"A Mr. Porlock and what looks like a Mrs. Gilford," Kyle, who had had difficulties reading Nina's handwriting, replied.

"Any addresses?"

"Yes; both London. 7 Harlow Gardens, NW3 for Mrs. Gilford and 19 Coleridge Avenue, SW6 for Mr. Porlock."

To the surprise of both Kyle and Boyce, Rudd, smiling broadly, began to intone, " 'Beware! Beware! His flashing eyes and floating hair!' " He broke off to explain, " 'Kubla Kahn' by Samuel T. Coleridge. What's the matter with you two? Didn't you read it at school? The pleasure dome of ice and Alph, the sacred river? I had to copy the whole damned thing out once in full because I laughed at that bit. I had an uncle Alf who was the most profane old blasphemer you'd ever want to meet. The point is, Coleridge was interrupted in writing the poem by the arrival of a man from Porlock. I think we've found ourselves a joker there."

"Who isn't going to be easy to trace," Boyce pointed out gloomily. "Not if he's given a false name and probably a false address as well."

"But we should be able to get his prints off the page," Rudd said, looking on the bright side. "Get the book bagged up, Kyle, and entered on the exhibits' register, then join the others in searching the garden. And when you write up your report, I want a full list of all the names and addresses."

As Kyle left, Rudd went towards the door, remarking to Boyce over his shoulder, "Come on, Tom. We'll let the experts get on with it for a couple of hours."

"Where are we off to?" Boyce asked, following Rudd along

the hall where the Chief Inspector paused on the doorstep to breathe in tangy autumn air, spiced with the bitter odour of burning leaves from someone's bonfire.

"To have a chat with Ambrose Scott who found the body. I want to know what he was doing calling on Miss Kershaw at twenty past eight in the morning. A bit early for paying a social visit, wouldn't you say?"

"Want to take the car?" Boyce asked.

"No, we'll walk," Rudd replied, setting off down the path. "Nice morning like this, it'll do us good. Besides, I want to take a look round at the area. We'll get a better idea on foot."

It was only when they were half-way down Church Crescent that Boyce remembered the question he had meant to ask earlier, and which had been nagging away at the back of his mind ever since.

"What did you mean by it looking more like a break-out than a break-in?"

Rudd turned to smile at him.

"Remember the French windows, Tom? The desk was placed at right angles to them, leaving very little room for the left-hand leaf of the doors to open back. In fact, it couldn't be swung fully open without banging against the corner of the desk. And yet we're supposed to believe that some random burglar comes up to the back of the house, forces the lock and then bursts both sections of the French windows open with sufficient force to pull the bolts away from the frame, but evidently without smashing the left-hand leaf against the desk and shattering the glass. If that's what happened, how did our supposed burglar manage it? The curtains were drawn so he couldn't have seen there was a desk just inside the room. I think those French doors were broken open after Miss Kershaw was murdered. And if that's the case, how the hell did he get into the house? There was no sign that any windows had been broken open. The back door was still locked and bolted when we examined it. Which leaves the front door, and as that wasn't forced, I think there's only one conclusion we can come to."

"Miss Kershaw let her killer in herself?"

"That's my opinion," Rudd agreed cheerfully as they turned into the High Street by All Hallows, just as the church clock was striking twelve.

CHAPTER SIX

They passed the gate to the churchyard just as Nina, gathering up her umbrella and handbag, prepared to leave, in search of the local police station before finding somewhere to have lunch. Not the hotel, she decided. It would be too recent a reminder of Miss Kershaw's death and her own shocked reaction to it.

The familiarity of the two figures walking a little ahead of her along the pavement—one stocky, the other tall and broad-shouldered—was also a shock, although after that first moment of astonished consternation, Nina could see the inevitability of the presence in Selhaven of the Chief Inspector and his Sergeant.

As for Rudd, the sound of a woman's voice calling his name was totally unexpected. So, too, when he turned round, was the sight of Nina Gifford hurrying to catch up with him and Boyce.

She had altered in the six years since he had last seen her at Althorpe. She had lost weight and her face seemed thinner and more angular; older, in other words. But it wasn't simply a matter of age. There was a new sophisticated air about her. She was better dressed, a neat grey skirt and jacket replacing the crumpled cotton dress which she had worn at their last meeting and her hair, instead of tumbling untidily from under the red-spotted scarf which she had tied gypsy-fashion over her head, was drawn back into some sort of coil; Rudd was never very good at women's hair-styles.

But, as she ran the last few steps towards them, some tendrils came flopping loose over her forehead. She put up a hand to dash them away with an impatient gesture which reminded him of the old, impulsive Nina, whom he had known and to whom, God help him, he had been so strongly attracted.

The memory added to his embarrassment, largely because until that moment he had forgotten about it. Since that time at Althorpe, he had fallen in love with someone else, proposed and been turned down. He liked to think he had come to terms with the rejection by building round it a containing wall of work and routine, and contact with those colleagues whom he regarded as friends, even though they knew nothing of his relationship with Marion Greave.

Seeing Nina Gifford reminded him painfully of the strength of physical attraction, that quick jolt to the senses that seemed to oxygenate the blood.

He also felt at a loss as to how to greet her, remembering the circumstances of their last encounter. Should he refer to Max Gifford? he wondered. Or was it better to pretend to forget the past and the part Rudd had played in that particular tragedy? It seemed to hang over her still, for as he smiled and held out his hand, he was aware of an anxious, strained look in her eyes.

He said, "Mrs. Gifford! How extraordinary to meet you here."

Without responding to his greeting, Nina plunged breathlessly into her account.

"I was going round to the local police station to speak to someone there. Then I saw you. It's about Miss Kershaw. I was there yesterday, at the museum. . . ."

Rudd made the connection in much the same way, he imagined, as she had realised, on seeing him and Boyce, that their reason for being in Selhaven was to investigate Miss Kershaw's murder.

"Yes, of course," he said. "One of my Detective Constables saw your name in the visitors' book."

He didn't bother to add that Kyle had misread it as Gilford, otherwise Rudd might have been aware earlier of the significance of the name, although he would most probably have dismissed it as a mere coincidence.

Seeing that the traffic lights on the corner had changed to red, he took her by the elbow, steering her across the road towards the Star public house opposite, and remarked, "Have you had lunch yet? No? Then let's talk over a drink and something to eat."

Inside the pub, he caught Boyce's glance and jerked his head at him, indicating to the Sergeant to make himself scarce. Taking the hint, Boyce went off by himself to the far end of the bar, leaving Rudd, after consulting Nina, to order two beef salads, a gin and tonic for her and a pint of bitter for himself, which he carried over to the table by the window where he had already installed her.

Nina watched him as he returned from the bar with the drinks. He had changed, she thought, but not physically so much. He still wore the same cheerful, open expression, and that air of guilelessness which she knew, from her previous encounter with him, hid a shrewd and watchful intelligence. But, observant herself, Nina sensed an underlying sadness about him, which she hadn't been aware of before and which, having experienced her own loss over Max, she immediately recognised.

I bet it's some woman, she told herself.

"Cheers!" she said out loud, smiling and picking up her glass.

Rudd hitched his chair nearer to hers. While he was at the bar ordering, he had come to a decision. He would begin casually, asking her what she knew about Miss Kershaw, and skirting round, at least for the time being, the more personal—and, he guessed, the more painful—subject of her private life since Max Gifford's death.

"So you were at the museum yesterday," he said.

Nina needed little encouragement. While she had been sitting in the churchyard, she had gone over in her mind what she would say to the police, not expecting that she would give her account to Rudd, of all people. And yet, in a strange way, it was easier. Even at Althorpe, he had been a good listener—part of his job, she supposed wryly.

She was half-way through her account of Mr. Porlock when the barmaid came across to the table with their beef salads and Rudd took the opportunity of the interruption to ask a few questions.

"What did this Mr. Porlock look like?"

"Small. Plump. Grey hair, balding at the back." Nina sketched him in the air with her fork, very much, Rudd imagined, as Max Gifford might have picked up a pencil to make a quick likeness.

"And you say he was interested in the Palmer drawing? Whereabouts in the museum was it hanging?"

"On the left of that big portrait of William Kershaw over the fireplace."

He'd have to check that the drawing was still there when he went back to the museum, Rudd thought.

"Valuable, is it?" he asked out loud.

"Yes; could be worth quite a lot to a collector, I should think, if it came up for auction," Nina replied, "although it'd depend on who else was interested in buying."

She didn't say and he didn't ask where she'd gained such knowledge. It was obvious to both of them.

"And you were saying you saw Mr. Porlock again later? When was this?"

It was at this point that they had been interrupted by the arrival of the barmaid with their salads.

"Yesterday afternoon. I realised I'd lost one of my ear-rings so I went back to the museum after lunch to see if I'd dropped it there. I'd just got up to the front door when I could hear Miss Kershaw quarrelling with a man." She broke off to ask, "Shall I tell you about that now or do you want me to go on about Mr. Porlock?"

It was said with the same directness, almost naivety, which Rudd remembered he had found attractive about her before.

"Keep to Mr. Porlock for the time being. We can pick up on the quarrel later."

"Well," Nina said, taking a breath, "it was a bit embarrassing so I decided to walk about for a bit and go back to the museum later. I went down by the river. There's an antique shop there, near where all the boats are anchored. I was looking in the window when I saw Mr. Porlock inside with the owner."

"Did he see you?"

"I don't think so. I cleared off. There was a painting in the window; not very good but that's neither here nor there. The point is," Nina went on, "I'm sure it's an art dealer's as well as an antique shop."

She stopped to let Rudd grasp the significance of her comment, and was disappointed when all he said was, "Tell me about the quarrel."

"I can't remember it word for word," Nina confessed.

"That doesn't matter. Just the gist of it will do."

"It seemed to be about William Kershaw. The man said she was being a fool and Miss Kershaw said it was none of his business. It was some decision she'd come to about her brother's books. At least, that's the impression I got."

"You didn't see the man?"

"No; they were inside the house, in Miss Kershaw's sitting-room, as a matter of fact, but both doors were open which was why I was able to hear them. Miss Kershaw said something to the man about him being one of William's oldest friends and she used his name. Oh, God, what was it? Began with an A. Unusual, too. I remember thinking at the time, you don't hear that name very often."

"Was it Ambrose?" Rudd suggested.

Nina widened her eyes at him.

"Yes, that's it! Have you met him?"

"Not yet. His name's cropped up though."

Rudd left it there, preferring not to explain how Ambrose Scott had entered the investigation through his discovery of Miss Kershaw's body. So far, as if by an unspoken agreement, both he and Nina had managed to avoid the reason why they were sitting there discussing her movements of the previous day.

"Was anything else said?" Rudd asked.

"Only that the man, Ambrose, said that a girl called Lucy had given Miss Kershaw the idea, whatever it was they were arguing about. And she, Miss Kershaw, I mean, said she made up her own mind although she admitted she'd been encouraged by Lucy's appreciating William's books. I didn't hear any more. But I saw her later when I went back to the museum."

"Miss Kershaw?" Rudd asked, momentarily losing his way in Nina's account among the thicket of personal pronouns.

"Yes; but I met the girl as well—Lucy; Lucy Blake, to give her her full name. Miss Kershaw introduced us. She called round for tea while I was there and returned one of William Kershaw's books she'd borrowed. She was going on and on about how good it was. I didn't like her."

"Why?"

Nina wrinkled her nose, partly in concentration, partly in remembered distaste.

"She was young and attractive but a damned sight too sure of herself; too clever by half. And I felt she was having Miss Kershaw on."

"What about?"

"William's books mainly. 'Super*b* ending! *Mar*vellous descriptions!' " Nina assumed a gushing, educated voice, repeating not only Lucy Blake's words but also, Rudd suspected, mimicking her accent and that quality of over-enthusiasm to which Nina had evidently taken exception. It was probably exaggerated, but he felt she had caught, if not the whole truth of the exchange, at least its spirit.

"It was odd, though," Nina continued, reverting to her normal voice, "that Miss Kershaw didn't realise what a right little bitch Lucy Blake was. She was no fool, Miss Kershaw. Very brisk and capable, I'd've said. And yet she seemed to have a blind spot about anything to do with her brother. You've seen the museum, of course? Well, there you are then," Nina concluded, as if nothing more needed to be said on the subject.

In the small silence after she finished her account, Rudd thought about Danny Webb, Nina's brother, whom he had met during the investigation at Althorpe. Like Imogen Kershaw, Nina was no fool either, and yet both women appeared to share an inability to be objective about any shortcomings in their respective brothers. The unspoken question of how Miss Kershaw had died also hung in the air between them. But Rudd felt it was not the occasion to voice it out loud.

Instead, he remarked, "I'll have to have a written statement from you, Mrs. Gifford. How long are you staying in Selhaven?"

"Only till tomorrow. I'm booked in at the King's Head on one of those cheap mid-week breaks."

"So you're just visiting?"

The momentum of their conversation was beginning to slow down now that Nina's account was completed, a fact which both of them were aware of. It was as if they were both circling round a forbidden territory, a Tom Tiddler's ground of taboos and prohibitions, neither of them wanting to be the first to put a foot across the boundary line.

And then Nina thought, Oh, sod it! and plunged in.

She said, "I came down here to look at the house where Max and I used to live, God knows why."

Which was only a half-truth. She had her suspicions about her motives, even if she hadn't cared to examine them too closely.

"But you haven't been there yet?" Rudd asked, guessing as much from the tone of her voice.

Nina shrugged and smiled, trying to make light of the situation, although Rudd saw her blink rapidly several times.

"Oh, you know how it is. There's no direct bus any more to Althorpe and then yesterday morning it rained and I got caught in it which was why I went to look round the museum. And then this morning, they were talking in the hotel about Miss Kershaw and somehow I hadn't got the heart to go after that. But it's not the end of the world. I can always come down again some other time."

On impulse, Rudd said, "I could drive you over there tomorrow morning in the car, if you like."

God knows how he'd manage it in the middle of a murder inquiry, but he'd find the time somehow. It wouldn't take much more than an hour anyway; twenty minutes there, twenty back —half an hour, say, at the house itself. And if he needed an excuse, he could always say that as Nina was a major witness, he wanted to go over her statement with her in more detail.

Nina was saying, "Would you really? I mean, I don't want to put you to any trouble."

"I'll pick you up outside the hotel at ten," he told her, getting up from the table.

They parted on the steps of the pub, and Nina walked away towards the hotel. Rudd turned back to beckon to Boyce, who was still propped up at the bar, filling in time by chatting up the barmaid while he had his own lunch of beer and cheese sandwiches.

They had barely got outside when Boyce made the inevitable comment.

"My God, fancy seeing her here! It must be—what?—all of six years since the Gifford case."

"Yes," Rudd said shortly, hoping to dissuade the Sergeant from blundering into that forbidden territory, on which he and Nina Gifford had so delicately avoided trespassing.

But the hint went unnoticed.

Boyce was saying, "What was the name of that bloke Gifford murdered? Hang on a minute, I've got it on the tip of my tongue. Quinn, something. Ernest? No; Eustace. That was it. An art-dealer, wasn't he? Gifford clobbered him over the head and then shot himself in the summerhouse over at Althorpe. Odd case, that."

It was not the epithet Rudd would have chosen to describe it.

He had a brief, vivid memory of interviewing Max Gifford not long before his suicide. He had been in bed, crippled with arthritis, his swollen hands resting on the covers but still giving, even then, an impression of the vigorous and passionate artist with whom Nina had fallen in love, and whom she had protected with such a fierce loyalty.

And probably still did. Rudd could not imagine Nina had ever fallen out of love with Max, even after his death.

Like him with Marion, he supposed wryly. They were two of a kind, he and Nina, which was probably why he found her attractive. A one-man woman and a one-woman man. Bloody ironic, wasn't it?

To shut Boyce up and to save himself from having to hear the Sergeant's version of the case, he said, more brusquely than he intended, "Quinn wanted to put on a retrospective exhibition of Gifford's paintings in London and Gifford was worried that he'd find out about his past. Quinn had been nosing about, asking questions. There'd been a model who'd sat for Gifford years before, and who he'd had an affair with—Lilith, he called her. She also happened to be Nina's mother, and Gifford was afraid Nina was his daughter; wrongly, as it turned out. But that's why he never married Nina. It was to keep the truth from her that he murdered Quinn."

"So what's she doing down here?" Boyce asked.

"Visiting friends, I gather," Rudd lied. He had no intention of explaining Nina's real purpose in coming to Selhaven, nor of discussing his promise to drive her over to Althorpe the following morning. He added quickly, to divert Boyce's attention, "You realise she went to the Kershaw museum yesterday morning? That's why I wanted to talk to her. And she came up with some very interesting information."

As they were speaking, they had turned off the High Street, following Bayliss's directions for Liston Road, and Rudd used the time to give Boyce a quick resumé of Nina Gifford's evidence as they walked. He broke off as they reached the gate to Ambrose Scott's house where Rudd paused, his hand on the latch, to glance up at its facade.

It was a small, undistinguished-looking Edwardian villa, built of red brick and with a disproportionately large gable and square bay windows. The porch, supported on posts and decorated with a finial and a border of fretted wood, also looked as if it had been designed for a much grander building.

Rudd pushed open the gate, and together he and Boyce tramped up the tiled path, past a small garden enclosed in privet, to the front door where the Chief Inspector rang the bell.

CHAPTER SEVEN

Ambrose Scott had been waiting nervously for the arrival of the police all morning. Even so, he wasn't entirely prepared for the presence of the two men in plain clothes on his doorstep, especially the shorter of the pair—who introduced himself as Detective Chief Inspector Rudd and who appeared to be in charge. He looked so disconcertingly unlike Ambrose Scott's conception of a professional detective that his first impression was of profound relief.

It was a feeling which persisted during the first part of the interview, which Rudd conducted in a comfortable, chatty manner, sitting relaxed amongst the books and strewn possessions in Ambrose's small sitting-room. He seemed perfectly at home, although had he known, Ambrose would have been taken aback by the speed with which, in those first moments, the Chief Inspector had summed up both the room and its owner.

It was a bachelor's or widower's quarters, Rudd suspected. No woman would have tolerated its untidiness. It seemed buttressed with books, which not only filled the shelves but stood in dusty piles on the furniture and about the floor. Scott had even had to snatch some up from the chairs before he and Boyce could sit down.

As for Scott, he had the same dishevelled appearance as his surroundings, as if no-one had bothered to give him a good dust and tidy up either. Awkwardly put together, he sat folded up in his armchair like a badly jointed wooden measure, all angles and corners, bony hands grasping his knees, elbows poking out sideways, his head, with its rumpled grey hair, thrust forward towards the Chief Inspector.

He exuded anxiety, and for this reason Rudd began easily, avoiding the more emotive subject of Scott's discovery of Miss Kershaw's body.

"Tell me about the museum. Has it been open for long?"

The question had its looked-for effect. Scott plunged straight into an account, eager to explain, eager to talk about anything rather than the murder.

He spoke surprisingly fluently, using his hands to emphasise his remarks in jerky movements, which nevertheless possessed an awkward eloquence of their own.

"About seven years ago, after William's death. You know a little about him, do you? He was a writer; a poet as well although not so good a poet as a novelist, at least in my opinion. Unfortunately, he's gone out of fashion these days. He was best known in the sixties, part of the finding one's roots movement—self-sufficiency, back to the countryside and all that. Remember it? William's books struck quite a chord at the time."

"You'd known him for long?" Rudd ventured as if it were a lucky guess and he hadn't already learnt this fact from his interview with Nina Gifford.

"Oh, Lord, yes; years and years," Scott agreed, jerking his hands apart to indicate the length of time. "We were at Cambridge together just before the war. William lived in Highgate at the time and, after he came down, he began teaching in a boys' private school nearby. Then at the start of the war he was sent to this area to do farm-work. He was C3, you see—unfit for active service. That's when he got keen on the countryside and started to write seriously. After the war, he sold up the Highgate home and he and his sister bought the house in Church Crescent. Clive and I used to visit them frequently."

"Clive?"

The name was new to the Chief Inspector.

"Clive Osborne, another of William's Cambridge friends. The three of us were quite inseparable. That was why, when I retired early from the Civil Service on health grounds, I decided to move down here. Clive was already settled in Selhaven. He'd married a girl he'd met when he was down here one week-end staying with William—Laura Bartlett; daughter, as a matter of fact, of John Bartlett of Bartlett and Drew's, the estate agent's. Heard of them, have you?"

"Indeed I have," Rudd replied. It was difficult not to be aware of the firm which had branches all over Essex. It would appear that Clive Osborne had made a very fortunate marriage.

"Her father kept a boat down here. That's how they met," Scott added in explanation, but with an odd note of apology in his voice which Rudd couldn't account for. "Anyway, as I was saying," he went on more briskly, "with Clive and William already living down here, it seemed sensible to move to Selhaven myself. There was nothing to keep me in London and I'd grown fond of the place over the years I'd been visiting William."

So far, Rudd noticed, there had been very little reference to Imogen Kershaw. Ambrose Scott's account had been centred largely on her brother William. Any other remarks concerning Clive Osborne or Scott himself were related to Kershaw as if, even seven years after his death, William Kershaw still dominated the small circle of his friends.

And his sister, too, Rudd imagined, recalling the house in Church Crescent, almost entirely given over to Kershaw's memory. It did not surprise him. The large photograph of Kershaw he had seen hanging in the museum had suggested a confident personality—self-assured, perhaps even a little overbearing; a man of strong opinions but evidently capable of inspiring devotion in those close to him. Rudd could picture him coming into a room and immediately taking charge of the conversation, very much in the same manner as he appeared to be directing Ambrose Scott's.

"Tell me about his sister," Rudd suggested.

He was aware of the sudden stillness that came over Scott as he made the request. From his former jerky animation, Scott became instantly immobile, fixed in his chair, his hands grasping his knees.

Then he said abruptly, "What do you want to know?"

"Well," Rudd replied in a casual voice, "you must have known her almost as long as her brother. What was she like?"

"Imogen?" Scott screwed up his eyes as if he were peering down the wrong end of a telescope at a figure that was very small and very far away. "She was a down-to-earth, sensible person, practical; no nonsense about her. What else do you want me to say?"

A damn sight more than that, Rudd thought.

The interview had come almost to a halt. From now on, it was going to be a question and answer session in which he extracted the information from Scott fact by fact. Like drawing teeth.

His experience told him that he'd do better to start with the past, slowly edging Scott towards the more recent events of that morning. To jump in feet first could be disastrous.

So he said, "She must have been quite a bit younger than her brother?"

"Six years," Scott replied.

"And I imagine she'd kept house for him. For how long?"

The sympathetic interest in his voice wasn't entirely feigned. Rudd himself had been in much the same position, cared for by a sister; in his case she was older than he. It was only in the past four years since her remarriage that he had properly appreciated all that she had done for him.

To his relief, Scott's hands began to stir again, releasing their tight grip of his knees and coming together in a cupped gesture which was oddly revealing, as if the man were holding something small and precious between his palms.

Seeing it, Rudd was convinced that Scott had been in love with Imogen Kershaw—probably for years, and almost certainly without having declared himself to her. It would have been typical of the man and his awkward reticence to have remained silent, an attitude which the Chief Inspector could understand. He himself had hesitated for a long time before proposing to Marion Greave, out of fear of rejection—justified, in his case.

Scott was saying, "She'd looked after William ever since she left school; even before that, in fact. The mother had died in the early thirties and Imogen more or less took over the running of the house. Old Mr. Kershaw was still alive but ailing. He died soon after the beginning of the war. Then, as I said, William was sent to a farm at Tolstead, just outside Selhaven. Imogen came with him. She was about seventeen then and he could hardly leave her alone in London, not once the blitz began. He rented a cottage in the village where he was working, and Imogen got a job with the Ministry of Food here in Selhaven, dealing with ration books and that sort of thing. She did a typing course as well at night school, so that she could help William with his writing. It was at that time he began his first novel. Clive and I always used to spend part of our army leaves with them. Then once William's books began to sell and they moved into Church Crescent, Imogen acted as his full-time secretary."

"It sounds as if she was very fond of her brother," Rudd suggested.

"Oh, devoted," Scott assured him. "Utterly devoted."

He spoke with a quick eagerness, and with that same look of peering intensity in his eyes, which convinced Rudd that his earlier supposition had been correct. Scott had been in love with Imogen Kershaw—utterly devoted, to use the same words as Scott himself in describing Imogen's relationship with her brother. And what chance had he stood, poor devil, in the face of that sisterly affection? Damn all, it would appear. Rudd began to feel sorry for the ungainly, rumpled man occupying the chair opposite him.

But sorry or not, he had to bring the interview to a conclusion, and he said, "Tell me about this morning. What made you go to the museum so early?"

Ambrose Scott immediately became motionless again, hands clutching his knees as if the contact gave him strength and comfort.

"I was worried about her. I'd tried phoning her a couple of times last night but there was no answer. At first, I wasn't too concerned. She could have been working on William's papers, in which case she'd simply ignore the phone."

"What time did you make the calls?"

Scott took a bolting look at the Chief Inspector and then at Boyce who, now that the interview was getting down to the facts of the case, had quietly produced his notebook from his pocket.

"The first was at about half past eight, I think. I tried again at a quarter to ten. I remember looking at the clock so I'm sure about the timing of that one. As she still didn't answer, I rang Clive, only his housekeeper told me he wasn't back from London. I was worried about her, you see."

This repetition by Scott of his concern struck Rudd as significant. Most people's reactions, after having twice tried unsuccessfully to call a friend, would be annoyance or frustration, not the obviously deep anxiety which Scott expressed. After all, quarter to ten wasn't that late, and as Scott himself had said, it seemed Miss Kershaw was in the habit of ignoring the phone if she were busy.

He put the question to Scott.

"Why were you so anxious to get in touch with her?"

Scott's grasp on his knees tightened.

"I wanted to apologise. I'd had an argument with her earlier in the afternoon."

"Did you?" Rudd's expression was perfectly bland, as if this were the first time he'd heard of the quarrel. "What was it about?"

"Is this really relevant?" Scott protested. When Rudd, instead of replying, cocked an inquiring eyebrow, he continued reluctantly, "Oh, very well. If you insist. It was about William's novels. Imogen rang me at lunch-time and asked me to go round to the house. She said she wanted to discuss something with me which she didn't want to explain over the phone. I called later, at about half past two. She said she was thinking of writing to various publishers suggesting William's books should be republished."

"Would any of them have been interested?" Rudd asked.

"Of course not!" Scott's voice rose; his hands also jerked upwards, making flapping gestures as if shooing away the whole idea. "It was a foolish scheme and I told her so. Perhaps I shouldn't have done but I wanted to save her the disappointment of being turned down."

"You said earlier that Miss Kershaw was a very sensible person so it doesn't sound like her. Could someone have put her up to it?" Rudd asked with an innocent air.

Even so, Scott was too intelligent not to be suspicious.

"You've heard of Lucy Blake?" he demanded.

Rudd shook his head, but instead of denying his knowledge of her outright, he merely said, "Tell me about her."

"I only met her once so I don't know a great deal except what I've heard from Imogen."

"Do you know where she lives?"

"No; except it's somewhere in Selhaven. Imogen became friendly with her about a year ago. It seems she visited the museum one afternoon, expressed an interest in William's books and ever since has been calling there regularly. Imogen took to her, something she rarely does—did, rather," Scott corrected himself hastily.

"Why?"

"For William's sake, mostly, as far as I could make out. Like William, Lucy Blake had been to University—London, I think —where she'd read English but had to leave because she'd had some sort of breakdown. Imogen was always impressed by anyone who'd had a 'varsity education.' She also told Imogen that she wanted to be a writer. There was another parallel as well. William had also had a nervous breakdown, in his case after he left Cambridge and was teaching in Highgate. It was the main reason he wasn't called up during the war for active service. And, of course, Lucy was very enthusiastic about William's books. She and Imogen used to discuss them. I'm not saying Lucy Blake suggested they should be republished. Imogen was too much her own person to take that sort of advice from other people. But I'm damned sure, if that girl hadn't been so keen, the idea wouldn't have occurred to Imogen in the first place.

"She'd some other scheme in mind as well. I left a message

with Clive's housekeeper asking him to ring me back when he got in. He phoned about quarter to eleven, I suppose, soon after he arrived home off the train, and told me that Imogen was thinking of getting the novels printed privately if she couldn't find a publisher who was interested in taking them, although God knows how she thought she'd find the money to pay for it. Imogen didn't mention it to me, probably because I'd been so unsympathetic about her idea of writing to the publishers. Clive'll be able to give you more details about that and about Imogen's financial affairs as well. He helped her with advice over her accounts after William died."

As he made the last remark, there was the same apologetic note in Scott's voice as he had used when speaking of Osborne's marriage, which prompted Rudd to ask, "But not before Kershaw's death?"

Scott looked unhappy.

"I'm afraid Clive and William had been estranged for a good many years. I don't think there was any quarrel as such; they just seemed to grow apart. It wasn't anybody's fault. Of course, Clive was very busy. After his marriage, he was taken into the family firm; did rather well, as a matter of fact—became one of the directors after old Bartlett's death. William, too, didn't help. He made no effort to mix with Clive's new business friends. He despised what he called the members of the 'cashocracy'; said they smelt of money. I could understand Clive's point of view. As he got older, William became more and more eccentric; hardly the sort of person to invite to a dinner party." He gave a sudden abrupt laugh, like the caw of some great bird. "And to be frank, Clive's wife was rather a snob. I think she discouraged the friendship. But there can't have been too many hard feelings. In his will, William appointed Clive as well as me as his literary executor and Clive went to his funeral. And, as I said, after William died—and Clive's wife, too—Clive and Imogen have been on very friendly terms."

"Did Miss Kershaw leave a will?" Rudd asked, wondering who

out of the circle of Imogen Kershaw's friends was likely to bene-fit from her death.

"I imagine so. Imogen was quite practical where that sort of thing was concerned. But Clive is the best person to ask. I be-lieve he introduced her to his solicitor."

"When was the last time you tried phoning Miss Kershaw last night?" Rudd asked, steering the interview back to the events immediately preceding the murder.

"I didn't try again after the second attempt to get in touch with her," Scott replied. "I hung on for Clive to ring me and he advised me to wait. He was quite sure Imogen would eventually see sense. It was getting on for eleven by then; too late to phone her. She usually went to bed at about that time. So I—I went to bed myself."

There was a small hesitation as he spoke the last part of the sentence, followed by a silence in which Rudd waited for what-ever Scott had seemed about to add. But the man had evidently changed his mind, for he resumed his account, more diffidently this time. The knuckles of his hands bulged white and his eyes fixed on a point to the right of Rudd's shoulder, as if the words were written up there on the wall and he were reading them slowly and reluctantly. And never once in this part of his state-ment, Rudd noticed, did he refer to Imogen Kershaw by name.

"I rang her again this morning at eight o'clock. I knew she was usually up quite early and would be more likely to answer the phone. When there was still no reply, I decided to go round to the house. I was worried she might be ill. I couldn't get an answer either when I rang the front door-bell so I walked round to the back of the house. I tried the kitchen door but that was locked. It was then that I noticed the French windows had been forced." He broke off to demand in a sudden outburst, "Do you want me to go on? I found her. Isn't that enough?"

"I'm sorry," Rudd said. He meant it genuinely. All the same, part of him remained unmoved, observing Scott's reactions with a professional detachment. He was a man of strong emotions, Rudd judged, capable of quick changes of mood—the type of personality which a sudden excess of rage or jealousy might have prompted him to deliver those three heavy blows with the walking-stick, as Imogen Kershaw lay on the floor.

Out loud, he said, "I'm afraid I'm going to have to ask you some questions, Mr. Scott. We need to establish certain facts. Were the curtains closed over the French windows?"

"Partly. They were dragged to one side, I suppose when the lock was broken and the windows were pushed inwards. All the curtains to the downstairs rooms, including the museum, were always drawn at night."

"I assume you walked through the museum to get to the sitting-room? Did you touch anything?"

"No; nothing apart from one side of the windows which I had to open back in order to get in."

"And Miss Kershaw's body? Did you touch that or try to move it?"

"No. I didn't even go inside the room. I could see she was dead from the doorway. All I did was turn on the light."

"So the room was in darkness?"

"Yes."

"And the curtains drawn?"

"Yes. I noticed that as soon as I went up to the front door. I realised then that something had happened to her."

"What did you do next?"

"I rang the police."

"From the phone in the hall?"

"Yes."

"And then?"

"I went out to the front garden to wait. I didn't want to stay in the house."

"Using the front door? Was it bolted?"

Ambrose Scott paused to consider, that look of peering intensity again on his face.

"No, it wasn't. I would have remembered if I'd had to draw the bolts." He became suddenly animated, as if the relevance of this fact had only just occurred to him. "She usually locked and bolted all the doors quite early before she went upstairs to work on William's papers. She had her own desk in one of the bedrooms which she called the manuscript room. Everything to do with William's affairs was kept in there—letters, documents and so on. She became very security-conscious after there'd been several break-ins in the area a couple of years ago."

"And you think that's what happened in this case?" Rudd asked with a disingenuous air.

Scott looked at him sharply.

"Isn't it obvious, Chief Inspector? I think she disturbed someone who'd broken into the house and who panicked when she confronted him. He picked up one of William's walking-sticks from the hall and used it to kill her. He then smashed open the display cabinets and took whatever there was of value."

"Was there much?"

"Not a great deal. There were a few items of silver—William's cigarette case, for example, and a gold watch and chain which had belonged to his father. I don't know what's missing. I didn't stop to check. As soon as the police arrived and took my name and address, I came back here."

"Is there an inventory?"

"I don't know. There might be one among her papers."

"But you'd be able to tell what was missing?"

"Yes, if I looked." Ambrose Scott seemed to grasp the drift of the Chief Inspector's remarks, for he hoisted himself upright in his chair, his expression anguished. "You're not expecting me to go back to the house?"

"Only if it's necessary," Rudd assured him. "If it is, I'll let you know. I'll have to ask you to make a written statement anyway and to have your fingerprints taken; only for purposes of elimination, of course. We're setting up an incident room at the local police station so it can be done there." He waited a moment, head cocked, before asking, "There's nothing else you want to add, Mr. Scott?"

The reply came a little too quickly.

"No."

"But I bet you there is," Rudd remarked to Boyce when, shortly afterwards, the interview over, he and the Sergeant left the house and set off together to walk back to the town centre.

It would have gratified the Chief Inspector to know that after his departure, Ambrose Scott lingered in the hall, his hand still on the lock, watching as the two figures, their outlines distorted by the reeded glass in the front door, retreated down the path and turned out of the gate.

God knows why he hadn't told the Chief Inspector about his visit to Imogen's house the night before, although he comforted himself with the thought that it was unlikely Rudd would ever get to hear of it.

CHAPTER EIGHT

From the town centre, Rudd and Boyce turned in the direction of the river, strolling past the Barge public house towards the antique shop.

The tide was out and the wind, blowing straight across the mud-flats, had a cutting edge to it, sending the stay wires of the boats at anchor jingling like cowbells among a forest of slanting masts and rigging.

On the farther bank, the land stretched away, flat and feature-less towards a few distant farms, crouching low among the marshes in their own small protective clumps of trees. But on the far side of the river, man was an irrelevance. It was nature which dominated—the sluggish water running between the mud banks, the clumps of tough grass and sea-lavender, and, dominating it all, the sky which occupied three-quarters of the vista, drenching everything with a pale grey luminous light, which brought with it the tang and glitter of the sea.

It was on the nearer shore where man had established himself. Selhaven clambered up the sloping land behind a curve in the river, oddly compact at that distance—a small citadel composed of roof-tops and gable-ends, the square flint tower of All Hallows forming its acropolis.

As Nina had done, Rudd and Boyce lingered for a few moments outside the antique shop, ostensibly examining the painting displayed in the window, but assuring themselves that the place was empty. Having established that it was, they pushed open the door and entered, a brass bell hanging over the lintel giving warning of their arrival.

The interior was large and artfully lit, lamps and spotlights strategically placed so that the attention was immediately drawn to the choicest items. Even Rudd, who knew little about antiques—and demanded nothing more from his own surroundings than comfort and ease of cleaning—could appreciate the richly glowing patina on rosewood and walnut, or the elegance of a finely turned cabriole leg.

Here and there, as if to justify the shop's name, Harbour Antiques, some object with a nautical connection was on show. A model of a schooner in a glass case stood on top of a cabinet, several seascapes hung on the walls while, at the far end, a ship's figurehead in the shape of the naked torso of a woman, still bearing traces of gilt, jutted out above a curtained doorway—hair streaming backwards, breasts straining forward, her blank wooden eyes searching for some distant horizon.

The curtain below this effigy was suddenly swished to one side and the owner of the shop, Tony Wallingford—according to the name written up outside on the shop sign—made his entrance.

There were nautical touches about Wallingford's appearance as well, chiefly in the navy blue blazer he was wearing, with its brass buttons and indecipherably elaborate crest in gold braid on the breast pocket. A matching navy blue silk scarf, knotted with casual elegance in the open neck of a white shirt, also suggested a marine background.

But there any connection with the real sea ended.

It was difficult to imagine the pearl grey trousers or the quiff of fair hair keeping their immaculate crispness on board any boat.

He was a tall man, softly fleshed and languid in movement, and yet with a sharpness of observation. In the few moments it took him to emerge from behind the curtain, he had already summed up Rudd and Boyce, and discounted them as serious customers.

His query, "May I help you?" was dismissive almost to the point of superciliousness.

"I hope so," Rudd said cheerfully, introducing himself and Boyce and producing his ID card with a flourish. He was pleased to see the small, superior smile on Wallingford's face disappear, to be replaced by a much more guarded expression.

"Yes?" he said and waited.

He was clearly not going to be hustled into making any involuntary statement.

Rudd took a quick look at Boyce who, picking up the cue, moved in closer. His bulk—which before had seemed merely ill at ease amongst Wallingford's exquisite antiques—assumed a more menacing stance. Rudd himself preserved his air of smiling insouciance.

"I believe you had a customer in here yesterday afternoon; a short, rather plump gentleman who may have used the name Porlock," he said.

"Oh, really, I can't be expected to remember every one of my clients. There are so many," Wallingford replied, waving a hand as if to people the interior with crowds of potential buyers.

Still smiling, Rudd gazed about him, raising one shoulder to express disbelief at its emptiness.

"That's a pity," he said, sounding genuinely contrite. "In that case, I'm afraid we're going to have to put you to a lot of trouble, Mr. Wallingford—making statements, looking at Identikit pictures, having your books examined." He made the suggestions with a faint interrogative note in his voice, leaving the decision entirely to Wallingford, who climbed down, taking care not to appear to do so too quickly.

"Yesterday afternoon, you said?"

"A short, plump gentleman," Rudd reminded him.

Wallingford pursed his lips as if giving the description serious consideration.

Then he said, "May I ask what your inquiries are about? If it's connected with stolen antiques, I can assure you . . ."

"No," Rudd corrected him gently. "Not theft, Mr. Wallingford. Murder."

"Murder?" Wallingford's voice rose in shocked outrage, as if Rudd had been guilty of uttering an obscenity. "Then, in that case, Chief Inspector, I'm quite sure my client, Mr. . . . ," He broke off to demand sharply, "Whose murder?"

"A Miss Imogen Kershaw who kept a private museum in Selhaven. You may have heard of her?" Rudd suggested.

The effect on Wallingford was immediate and dramatic.

Pulling forward a lyre-backed chair, one of a set of six which, together with a Regency dining-table laid with china and silver, formed the centre-piece of the shop, he sat down heavily upon it, pushing aside Georgian cutlery and crystal wineglasses with his elbows as he put one hand over his eyes.

Above the quiff of his hair—curiously static as if it had been lacquered into place—Rudd and Boyce exchanged glances.

"You were saying?" Rudd asked, adding more impatiently when he received no response, "Now come on, Mr. Wallingford. You know who we mean. Are you going to tell us his name or are you going to close the shop and come with us to the police station to make a statement? It's up to you."

At this suggestion, Wallingford got abruptly to his feet, stalked across to the door, drew the bolts and turned the hanging sign in the glass panel to "Closed." He remained there for several moments to peer up and down the river-front, empty of anything except sea-gulls and an elderly man in wellington-boots and a woolly hat, emerging reluctantly from the door of the Barge at closing-time.

Then, turning to face the Chief Inspector and the Sergeant, like a man at bay facing his tormentors, he said, the whole surface of his face trembling, "Do I have to be dragged into this affair? I have a reputation to consider. I'm a member of the local Round Table, for God's sake. It could ruin me if my name were connected with anything so dreadful, so appallingly awful as . . ."

He stopped there, clearly finding it impossible to articulate the word "murder."

Rudd gestured towards the chair which Wallingford had vacated.

"I suggest you sit down again, Mr. Wallingford, and tell us

exactly what you know. It couldn't by any chance have something to do with a Samuel Palmer drawing, could it?"

Wallingford, who was half-way across the shop, stopped in his
tracks, aghast at this revelation.

"Oh, my God!" he said. "You know about the Palmer!"

"I know that a certain gentleman, calling himself Porlock,
although I doubt very much if that's his real name, was seen
yesterday morning at the Kershaw museum showing a great deal
of interest in the drawing. I also happen to know that the same
gentleman visited your shop later that afternoon. I just wondered,"—Rudd made the remark with the air of a man unwilling
to jump to any conclusions which might be detrimental to Wallingford's good name—"if the two facts might be connected and
could have any bearing on Miss Kershaw's murder."

Wallingford lowered himself gingerly onto the edge of the
chair, watching as Rudd and Boyce seated themselves on each
side of him, settling down as if they were in no hurry and had all
the time in the world to listen to Wallingford's account. Getting
out his notebook, Boyce turned to a clean page.

As the Sergeant did so, Wallingford began to talk, as if
Boyce's action had triggered some mechanism inside him which,
once set in motion, would not stop until it had run itself down.
He spoke so quickly that Boyce's pencil had difficulty in keeping
up with him.

"The man's name is Maurice Chadwick. He's a collector,
mainly of eighteenth and early nineteenth century English landscapes. He got in touch with me about a year ago, having seen
my advertisement in the Collectors' Guide, asking me to let him
know if I came across anything of that period. It's not strictly my
speciality although I deal, as you can see, in some paintings,
mainly seascapes. However, going round the auctions, one can
sometimes come across the occasional water-colour which might
be worth acquiring if one has a special buyer in mind. As soon as
I heard about the Palmer, I got in touch with Chadwick."

"And how did you come to hear about that particular drawing?" Rudd asked.

Wallingford, unwilling to divulge trade secrets, said warily, "A contact, Chief Inspector. Do I have to say more?"

"I need a name," Rudd told him.

"Oh, dear! Well, if you insist. It was a young woman."

"Attractive; fair-haired?" Rudd said, giving Nina's description of Lucy Blake.

"Attractive, yes, I suppose so." Wallingford conceded this point reluctantly. "Fair-haired, certainly. I'm afraid I don't know her name. I didn't ask although she lives in East Lane, just behind the Barge. I've noticed her coming out of the turning on occasions, sometimes with her boy-friend. I've seen him about, too; quite a lot. He owns a small cabin cruiser that's moored a little higher up the river; rather scruffy, to be honest."

"The boy-friend or the boat?" Rudd asked.

"Both," Wallingford said promptly. "Actually, the girl's educated and well-spoken. He's quite the other end of the market, if you know what I mean. But some young women prefer the rough trade, or so I've heard. I believe it's the fashion these days."

"Know anything else about them?" Boyce put in.

"Not much," Wallingford admitted. "He hires the boat out from time to time for fishing trips; owns a green van as well. I've seen him parking it outside the Barge. Being here in the shop, I have an excellent ringside seat for seeing who's coming and going."

"You said the young woman came into the shop? Why?"

"She brought in a piece of china to be valued; quite a nice little Worcester jug, as a matter of fact. I offered to buy it but she refused to sell. She said someone living in Selhaven had given it to her as a birthday present and she didn't want it to be put on sale in the shop in case the original owner recognised it. I recommended a colleague of mine who has a shop in Colchester and who might be interested in buying it."

"For a commission?" Rudd suggested, at which Wallingford looked pained.

"One has to live," he replied. "Anyway, I asked her if the person who had given her the china had anything else to dispose of. One never knows. It could have been the young woman's aunt or grandmother with a house stuffed full of God knows what. You'd be surprised what can turn up at even the most unpromising of places. She said the china had been given to her by a Miss Kershaw who ran a small private museum in the town and as most of the contents was part of the display, it was unlikely she'd want to part with anything."

"But you went along to have a look?"

"Good Lord, no, Chief Inspector!" Wallingford sounded shocked at the mere idea. "One has to go about these things much more circumspectly. I sent that chum of mine from Colchester round there to do a little recce on his half-closing day. He rang me that evening to say there was nothing much of interest to either of us apart from a drawing which he thought might be a Palmer. He couldn't be sure; the picture was unsigned and his speciality is china, not works of art."

"I assume this is where Mr. Chadwick came in?" Rudd suggested.

"I contacted him certainly," Wallingford agreed, "and suggested he took a look himself and, if the drawing were a genuine Palmer and he was interested in buying it, I'd do my best to acquire it on his behalf."

"How?"

"Oh, dear, dear, dear!" Wallingford's distress increased at the Chief Inspector's lack of finesse in these matters. "It would need very delicate handling. I understood the lady in question . . ."

"Miss Kershaw," Rudd put in, just to keep the record straight.

"Miss Kershaw," Wallingford agreed snappily, "was elderly and, according to the information given to me, was likely to be short of money. She might, if approached in the right manner, be willing to part with the drawing for, say, a couple of hundred pounds with certain other inducements."

"Such as?" Rudd asked, certain in his own mind that the anonymous person who had supplied Wallingford with his information was Lucy Blake.

Wallingford seemed to regret having made his remark about

inducements. A veiled expression came over his face and he began studiously to re-arrange the cutlery on the table.

"No exact plans had been made, Chief Inspector, but it was suggested that I might offer to mount a window display centred round William Kershaw's life—a few photographs and volumes of his work artistically set out, that sort of thing; perhaps even some of his own sketches although I gather they were quite dreadful."

A clever touch that on Lucy Blake's part, Rudd thought. If anything could persuade Miss Kershaw to part with the drawing, it would be a proposal to publicise her brother's books.

"So you contacted Mr. Chadwick," Rudd said, leading Wallingford back to the main issue, "and he called on you yesterday afternoon, having visited the museum in the morning. Tell me, was the drawing a genuine Palmer?"

Wallingford arranged a silver spoon just so on the polished surface of the table before replying.

"In his opinion, yes, it was."

Rudd got up from his chair.

"I'd like Mr. Chadwick's address and telephone number, Mr. Wallingford."

When Wallingford returned from his office at the rear of the shop, the information written down on the back of one of his business cards, Rudd glanced at it, noting it was a London address and then continued, "I think I should warn you not to contact Mr. Chadwick until my Sergeant and I have had a chance to interview him. I'm sure you wouldn't want to obstruct our inquiries. And I shall also need an official statement from you at some later stage, including an account of your movements yesterday evening."

"My movements? You mean an *alibi?* But I haven't got one! I went to the cinema last night on my own."

"Which one?"

"The Odeon in Colchester."

"Good film, was it?" Rudd asked conversationally, stowing away the card with Chadwick's address on it in his wallet.

Wallingford gave a small, embarrassed laugh as he escorted them across the shop.

"A western, Chief Inspector. Cowboy films are one of my little weaknesses. I do so love the saloon-bar fights." He paused at the door before drawing the bolts, to express a concern which was evidently more on his mind than his own lack of an alibi. "About the Palmer. I assume there'll be a sale of Miss Kershaw's effects now that she's—well," he coughed deprecatingly, "deceased. I wondered if the Palmer would be included. I mean, it's still there, isn't it? Nothing's happened to it?"

"I don't know," Rudd replied. "I shall have to take a look, won't I?"

But, on leaving the antique shop, his first concern was to examine the boats moored along the river bank. They were of assorted shapes and sizes, from small dinghies, lying as if abandoned on the mud, to the large sixty-foot sailing barges, a tangle of masts and rigging, their long bowsprits jutting out like battering rams.

It was the cabin cruisers which he looked over with the closest attention, many of them laid up for the winter, neatly lashed into their tarpaulin covers. He sauntered along, stopping at last in front of one, painted a dingy white, its deck uncovered, and with the name the "Lucy Fair" emblazoned along its bow in black letters on a faded blue flashing.

"Know anything about boats, Tom?" Rudd asked.

"Not a lot," Boyce admitted.

"Neither do I."

Rudd went on contemplating it for a few more moments, hands in pockets, and then turned away in the direction of the Barge and the narrow street which ran behind it.

The green van was clearly visible, parked half-way down East lane outside number fourteen. As they approached it, Boyce bent down to peer in at the driver's window and then shrugged, indicating there was nothing of interest inside. Rudd, waiting on the pavement, rang the bell.

The house must have been of flimsy construction. Even

through the front door, they could hear footsteps come thumping down the stairs. A moment later, the door was flung open and a young woman appeared on the threshold.

Had Nina been with them, she would have been surprised at the change in Lucy Blake's appearance. The demure black skirt and jumper had been replaced by jeans and a man's shirt, several sizes too large, worn loose like a jacket, the sleeves rolled up and the collar open. The petersham bow had also gone, and the mass of crinkly fair hair sprang loose about her head and shoulders in an unruly halo.

"Miss Blake?" Rudd inquired politely, although he didn't much care for the look of her. She was attractive all right, but there was a superior air about her, not just the impertinence of youth, which he could have tolerated—more the arrogance of privilege.

It was evident also in her voice, educated and disdainful.

"Yes, what do you want?" she demanded.

"Police," Rudd said, producing his ID. "We'd like a word with you."

He saw her expression harden.

"What about?"

"Miss Kershaw."

"Miss Kershaw?" A look of relief came briefly into her face. "What about Miss Kershaw?"

"Look," Rudd said pleasantly, "it's not something I want to discuss on the doorstep. Do you mind if we come in?"

She opened the door grudgingly, preceding them into a small sitting-room, where she did not invite them to sit down. Rudd tried not to look too pointedly at the squalor about him, although his gaze rested momentarily on a small jug, stuffed with sea-lavender, which stood on the mantelpiece among a clutter of other objects.

He was aware also of a distinctive odour in the room, sweetly stale, like musty flowers smouldering on a bonfire.

Boyce had registered it, too. Rudd saw him raise his head like a gun-dog scenting game.

Lucy Blake was saying impatiently, "Well, get to the point."

"I believe you visited the Kershaw museum yesterday afternoon," Rudd began.

"Yes, I did. I had tea with Miss Kershaw but I don't see that it's any of your damned business."

If that was her attitude, Rudd thought, it was none of his damned business either to bother with a softly-softly approach.

So he said outright, "The museum was broken into last night and Miss Kershaw was murdered."

"*What!*"

She could have feigned that look of astonished disbelief. Rudd wouldn't have put it past her. She had evidently fooled Miss Kershaw for nearly a year. But not Nina Gifford, it seemed. Full marks to her for perspicacity.

"I shall need an account of your movements yesterday evening," Rudd continued.

"Why mine?"

"Because we're checking on everyone who knew Miss Kershaw."

"But you said it was a burglary. Anybody could have done it."

Top marks to her as well. She was too intelligent not to pick up that point straight away.

"If you object," Rudd suggested with a smile.

It was like a game, each one trying to out-manoeuvre the other, but she was unlikely to win on this occasion. He held too many cards, one of which, his knowledge of the part she had played in the negotiations over the Palmer drawing, he decided not to reveal just yet.

She said, "I've no objections although I resent the implication. I was out last night with a friend at the Ring of Bells in Chelmsford."

"That's a long way to go for a drink."

"We happen to like it there."

Rudd let that one pass.

He said, "What time did you leave the pub?"

She shrugged.

"About ten o'clock, I suppose. Ask the landlord. He may have noticed."

"And your friend? I'd like a name and address."

"Jed—Gerald Kemp. And he lives here. With me," she added, in case Rudd hadn't got the point.

Rudd cocked his head towards the ceiling, from where he could hear the faint sound of floorboards creaking as someone moved about softly in an upstairs room.

"Could I have a chat with him?"

She had the effrontery to smile.

"He's not in at the moment. Hard luck."

"Never mind," Rudd said equably, going over to the door. "I'll take a statement from him some other time."

Once they had left, Jed came slamming down the stairs.

"Christ!" he exclaimed. "That was the bloody Bill, wasn't it? What the frig did they want?"

"Not what you think. It was about Miss Kershaw. She was murdered last night."

"Murdered? Bloody hell, Luce! Why should anyone want to do that?"

"God knows." She shrugged indifferently. "She was evidently killed by someone who broke into the museum." She paused, and when he didn't make the connection, she continued, "They want to take a statement from you. I told them we were at the Ring of Bells last night."

"What did you tell them that for?"

"Why not? It's the truth. And what's wrong with going out for a drink?"

Jed sat down on the sofa and put his head between his hands.

"You realise what this means? We're going to have to call off the bloody trip. I'll have to ring that number in London Doug gave me."

Lucy went to stand over him.

"Why?"

"Well, isn't it frigging obvious? We can't risk it, not with the fuzz nosing round."

PAST RECKONING

93

"They're not interested in anything except the murder. They're CID, Jed, not the other lot. Besides, we can't cancel. We waited six weeks for this drop. If we call it off, we may not get another one."

She gave him time to mull over the implications and at last, reluctantly, he raised his head.

"Yeah, you're right, Luce," he agreed. "Dead right, as usual. We're going to have to bloody chance it."

CHAPTER NINE

Rudd's first action on returning to the museum in Church Crescent was to check the Palmer drawing.

Kyle was hanging about in the hall, evidently keen to pass on some information to the Chief Inspector, but, telling him to wait, Rudd brushed past him. He crossed the room and made straight for the fireplace, at the side of which, according to Nina Gifford, the Palmer should have been found.

It had gone. Rudd could see from the lighter rectangle on the flowered paper where the picture had once hung.

Boyce observed helpfully, "It's not there."

Stuffing his hands in his pockets, Rudd went on staring at the oblong, as if expecting the missing drawing to materialise out of the wall. At times, Boyce could be infuriating.

Then, turning abruptly, he surveyed the room.

The SOCOs had moved in, having finished with Miss Kershaw's sitting-room. They had taken over the far end, where they were dusting the French windows and Kershaw's desk with aluminum powder, looking for prints. Beyond their bent heads, he could see through the glass the uniformed men still occupied with the search of the garden, which had now almost reached as far as the gate in the end wall.

Jerking his head at Boyce, he tramped back into the hall to speak to Kyle.

The young DC's information was quickly reported. A pair of gloves had been found in the garden. Did the Chief Inspector want to have a look at them before they were bagged up for forensic examination?

Rudd did, and with Kyle leading the way, the three of them

walked round by the side of the house to the back garden where, at a point half-way down on the right, Kyle pointed to an over-grown rhododendron bush.

"They're under there, sir," he said.

Rudd squatted down, breathing in the pungent odour of the shrub as he carefully parted the leaves. The ground below was dry, despite the rain of the previous day, and deep in old leaf litter. The gloves lay on top—placed there rather than thrown down, and still holding in the cupped form of their leather palms the contours of the hands which had been inside them. Their shape reminded him of Ambrose Scott. Scott's hands had come to rest in much the same position when he had spoken of Imogen Kershaw.

Addressing Kyle over his shoulder, Rudd asked, "Has McCullum photographed them?"

"Yes, he has, sir."

"And their position's been measured?"

On receiving Kyle's assurance that it had, Rudd leaned forward and, picking up a twig, gently lifted one of the gloves a few inches off the ground so that he could get a better look at it.

It was a man's glove, old-fashioned in style, the cuff fastening with a small metal stud. The brown leather of which it was made was so dry and hard that it had lost its flexibility, accounting for its retention of the shape of the hand which had last been inside it.

Almost before he saw the initials W. K. printed in Indian ink on the worn, fleecy lining, he had guessed where the gloves had come from. They had the look of relics rather than recent personal possessions, and it struck him as ironic that Miss Kershaw's killer had used her own brother's walking-stick and gloves in carrying out her murder. Suggestive, too. It meant that whoever had battered her to death hadn't come equipped for the crime, but had picked up whatever had been to hand.

He straightened up.

"No footprints, I suppose?" he asked, not with much hope. The grass round the bush was too long to take any imprints.

"Sorry, sir."

Kyle sounded defensive, as if the absence of such evidence was entirely his responsibility.

"All right. You can get them bagged up," the Chief Inspector told him before walking away down the garden towards the wooden door in the end wall. Stepping carefully past two more Scene of Crime officers, who were crouching over the half-moon of disturbed soil and crushed grass where the door had been forced open, he emerged, with Boyce at his heels, into a narrow alley which ran behind the back of the houses.

"So he must have come out this way," the Chief Inspector remarked, half to himself, "getting rid of the gloves as he went."

"Couldn't he have come in this way as well?" Boyce asked.

"Possible, but unlikely, according to the evidence, Tom. Scott told us Miss Kershaw was careful to bolt as well as lock both the back and front doors quite early in the evening and yet, when he found her body this morning, the front door was unbolted. Unless we assume she was murdered before it got dark, and I think that's improbable, it means she must have let her murderer in herself through the front door. He certainly didn't break his way in through the French windows, for the reasons I've already explained. That was done later, to make it look like a burglary that had gone wrong. And, if I'm right and she let her killer in, then there's only one likely explanation."

"That she knew who it was."

"I can't see her inviting a stranger into the house," Rudd replied. "Which points the finger at quite a small group of people—Ambrose Scott, Lucy Blake, Clive Osborne and anyone else she may have known well enough to open the door to, such as Maurice Chadwick, alias Mr. Porlock."

"Is he likely?" Boyce objected. "She hardly knew him. He was only a visitor to the museum."

"He could have called back; perhaps even made arrangements to see her later on some pretext or other. The same could apply to Wallingford. Even though he says he never met her, we only have his word for it. It's possible he'd visited the museum, perhaps more than once, and got to know her, rather as Lucy Blake did. Supposing he rang her yesterday and asked if he could call and see her?"

"It's a possibility," Boyce agreed. "He's got no proper alibi after all. And then there's the missing drawing. That could give him a motive."

"Yes, I'll need a full description of that from Mrs. Gifford," Rudd said, preparing the ground in case he should need an excuse for meeting her again the following morning. "If it's a genuine Palmer, as Wallingford said, it could be worth a few bob. We may have to circulate the dealers."

"It could account for the faked burglary," Boyce put in, warming to the idea. "Supposing, like you said, Wallingford turned up last night and tried to persuade her into selling the Palmer? There could have been an argument in which he killed her. He then decided to clear off with the drawing, smashing the cabinets and the French windows and helping himself to a few other bits and pieces at the same time so that nobody'd be suspicious it was only the Palmer he was interested in."

"Could be," Rudd said. "But there's still the others—Scott, Lucy Blake and Osborne. I'll have to interview him tomorrow. Then there's Chadwick. The fact that he signed the visitors' book with a false name and address looks suspicious. But apart from him, any one of the others could have had a motive. Certainly Scott had the opportunity. He was alone last night. Lucy Blake's alibi covers only the early part of the evening and that raises the whole question of timing. Scott said he telephoned Miss Kershaw at half past eight and again at a quarter to ten and there was no answer on both occasions. Now I know we've only got his word for it but, if he's speaking the truth, it's possible she was dead when he made that first call. Or she may simply have ignored the phone as he thought at the time. But whenever she was murdered, it can't have been all that late. She was still fully dressed. Again according to Scott, although we only have his say-so to go on for that as well, Miss Kershaw was in the habit of going to bed at eleven. We can try checking with the neighbours. Perhaps one of them will know something of her habits. Or Pardoe may be able to give us a more precise time of death. Which reminds me," he added, glancing at his watch, "I'm due at the PM this afternoon. Let's see where this alley leads to, Tom. After that, I want a quick look at the upstairs rooms before I push off to meet Pardoe."

The alley led into a residential road which ran at right angles to Church Crescent and which was lined with similar large, detached houses. Judging by the infrequency of the lampposts placed along the pavements, it would be poorly lit at night and was unlikely to be used by many passers-by. As for the residents, most of them would be indoors with their curtains drawn after dark.

As he pointed out to Boyce, anyone turning out of the alley from the back entrance of the museum had a good chance of getting away unseen.

Walking back along the alley towards the house, he turned over in his mind Boyce's earlier comments.

They made sense. If Rudd were right about the break-in being faked, and he was damned sure he was, then the Sergeant's theory—that the burglary itself had been used as a cover-up for the theft of one particular item, the Palmer drawing—would fit in with his own speculations.

And that would tend to throw suspicion onto three people: Lucy Blake, Wallingford and Chadwick.

He'd have to make arrangements to interview Chadwick in London as soon as possible, he decided, and have another talk with Lucy Blake. He'd also get one of the DCs to check up on her background.

There was another matter regarding Lucy Blake which he wanted to follow up as well. He could do that later after the PM.

Inside the house, he and Boyce put on protective coveralls and disposable plastic gloves and boots before mounting the stairs to examine the upper rooms, none of which had so far been examined by the SOCOs.

This part of the house seemed undisturbed. Opening a door to the left, immediately at the head of the stairs, Rudd revealed what he took to be William Kershaw's bedroom, judging by its masculine possessions. Miss Kershaw's was on the opposite side of the landing, also facing the front of the house. The curtains were still closed, he noticed, and the bed unslept in, confirming his suspicion that the murder had taken place in the early part of the evening.

The rest of the upper floor contained a spare room, furnished but unused, the bed stripped down to its mattress; a box-room, which might have been intended originally for a servant; a bleak, old-fashioned bathroom, still equipped with its deep bath raised on clawed feet and an iron lavatory cistern; and finally the fourth bedroom, which Ambrose Scott had referred to as the manuscript room.

The blind was drawn down over the window and the room was in darkness. As the SOCOs had not yet examined it, Rudd flicked on the overhead light with a biro in order not to smudge any prints which might be on the switch.

It was a bare room, unfurnished apart from a heavy oak desk and a swivel chair which stood under the window; both looked as if they might have been bought second-hand at an office-clearance sale. So might have the angled reading-lamp. As for the typewriter, it pre-dated even the lamp. It was one of those upright machines, weighty enough to take two strong men to lift it, with its metal innards unashamedly exposed—a collector's item itself.

The original bedroom fireplace was still in position, its flue blocked up with hardboard, a small electric heater on the hearth. The wallpaper hadn't been changed either, not that much of its ivy-leaf and trellis design could be seen for the shelves which lined the room. They in turn were filled with box-files, ledgers, cardboard cartons and manila folders, the front of each one docketed with a small, neatly typed label giving details of the contents.

Rudd glanced at some of them as he walked across the worn carpet towards the desk: "Memorabilia Tolstead 1941–1948,"

"Notebooks 1939–48," "Memorabilia Cambridge 1936–1939." He was vaguely aware that something was wrong, but unable for the moment to put his finger on it.

There was a whole wall of shelves given over to William Kershaw's manuscripts, the files containing them labelled not only with the titles of the books, but stating also whether they were first or second drafts, handwritten or in typescript.

The desk was arranged with the same orderly precision. Containers for pens, rubber bands and paper clips stood along the back while an opened packet of envelopes lay next to a small pile of A4 paper, a sheet of which protruded from the typewriter roller.

It was a letter, dated the previous day and addressed to the publishing firm of Holt and Webber.

Leaning forward, his hands clasped behind his back so that he would not be tempted to touch it, Rudd read:

"Dear Sir,

Although William Kershaw's books have been out of print for several years, I wondered if your firm would be interested in republishing at least some of the titles, bearing in mind that next year is the twentieth anniversary of the publication of his most successful novel 'The Bright' . . ."

At this point, the letter broke off.

"Interesting," Rudd commented to Boyce, who had come to stand behind him and read its contents over the Chief Inspector's shoulder. "It looks as if Miss Kershaw was interrupted and never went back to finishing it, perhaps because at that moment she had a visitor."

"Like that poet, what's his name, and the man from Porlock?" Boyce suggested with a grin.

"Exactly," he agreed. "But who called on Miss Kershaw and interrupted her in mid-sentence? And what happened next? Presumably she went downstairs to let her visitor in. . . ." He broke off to look across the room. "And first turned the light off in here? It was off when we came in. Or did she leave it on, intending to come back later in the evening to finish the letter and someone else switched it off? And if that was the case, why should anyone want to come upstairs?"

Boyce raised his shoulders, indicating it was anybody's guess.

But the gesture was lost on Rudd. He had moved away towards the shelves on the right of the desk where, after that first cursory glance, he had felt something was wrong.

The next moment, he was striding out of the room to shout down over the bannisters for one of the SOCOs.

"Wylie! Up here! And bring a lamp with you."

"What's up?" Boyce asked as Rudd returned.

"Take a look at this shelf, Tom. It's all Kershaw's personal stuff, letters, notebooks, memorabilia—presumably photographs and such-like. Notice anything about the files?"

"Can't say I do," Boyce replied, stooping to examine them.

"They're all in order of date except for the ones for Cambridge and Tolstead which was where, according to Scott, Kershaw did his war-work on a farm. Look at the labels." He stabbed a finger. " 'Tolstead 1941–48.' 'Cambridge 1936–39.' They should be the other way round."

"So Miss Kershaw put them back in the wrong order," Boyce said, in a tone suggesting the Chief Inspector was making a song and dance over nothing.

"No, not her. Look at the rest of the stuff in here. It's obsessively tidy." He broke off to give instructions to Wylie who had come into the room, holding a powerful hand-lamp. "Shine it along here. Can you see if anything's been disturbed?"

The beam of brilliant light, angled along the horizontal plane of the shelf, illuminated a faint fur of dust, scattered at the point where the two files were standing.

"They've been moved," Wylie said over his shoulder.

"Recently?"

"It looks like it. The dust hasn't had time to settle over the marks."

"Right," Rudd said. "I'll want McCullum to photograph those files but I don't want them touched or moved until I say so. Leave them exactly as they are for the time being."

"I'll let the others know," Wylie said and left the room.

"What's the idea?" Boyce asked.

"I want Scott to have a look at them. We'll have to get him over here soon anyway to check on what's missing downstairs," Rudd replied. He took another look at his watch. "Lord, is that the time? I'm going to be late for the PM."

He was a good three-quarters of an hour late, but not too late to miss the autopsy entirely.

Pardoe, in protective clothing and mask, glanced up as Rudd came sidling in round the swing doors.

He never felt entirely at ease in Pardoe's world of bright lights, stainless steel and rubber tubing. It was alien to him, although he supposed Marion Greave, a pathologist herself, would have found it familiar. For his own part, he was there out of duty—a part of his job that had to be carried out.

"I got held up," he said by way of an excuse, taking care to stand well back.

Pardoe waved him forward.

"Knowing you, I didn't hang about. Want to have a look?"

He sounded pleased with himself, as if the PM was a work of art, which perhaps in a way it was.

Rudd went over to the slab to peer down at the naked remains of Imogen Kershaw, feeling, as he always did on these occasions, like a voyeur. The face had been cleaned of blood, and the features which he hadn't been able to distinguish before with any clarity were revealed as thin-boned and delicate, the skin round the eyes netted with fine laughter lines, suggesting a sense of humour, although the set of the jaw and mouth, even in death, hinted at more stubborn qualities.

He hadn't realised how small she was. The torso was almost child-like in its proportions.

"As I thought, there were three heavy blows to the front of the skull," Pardoe was saying, pointing to where the thick grey hair had been shaved back to expose the wounds. "And a minor injury to the back of the head which could have been caused by her falling against the fender. No other injuries that I can see; no bruising, no marks on the hands; finger-nails unbroken and nothing of any interest under them."

"So she didn't defend herself," Rudd said.

"It doesn't look like it," Pardoe agreed.

Which would tie in with the theory that she knew her killer, Rudd thought.

Out loud, he said, "There's a problem over the timing. . . ."

"There always is," Pardoe interrupted. "And I'm afraid I can't help you much there. The rectal temperature and the degree of rigor mortis when I examined her this morning suggested she'd been dead about eleven to fourteen hours which would place the time she was killed between midnight and nine o'clock yesterday evening. And according to the lividity stains on the back and shoulders, she died where she fell. I haven't had time yet to open the stomach and have a look at the contents but if you want to wait, you're welcome."

"Sorry," Rudd said, not really meaning it. "I'll have to be shoving off. Can I use your phone?"

"Help yourself," Pardoe called after him as Rudd made for the swing doors.

In Pardoe's office, he dialled the number of Divisional Headquarters and asked to be put through to Detective Inspector Archer.

"Arch?" he said when the DI came to the phone. "It's Jack Rudd. Any chance of meeting me shortly for a drink?"

"Business or pleasure?"

"Business, mainly. What about the Castle in Broome Street?"

"Make it the Holly Bush. I use the Castle for chatting up one of my informers. Say in half an hour?"

"Fine by me," Rudd said and rang off.

Archer was in the bar waiting when the Chief Inspector arrived, a couple of pints already set out on the table in front of him.

"I got them in," he said in greeting, as Rudd slid onto the banquette seat beside him. "Your shout next time. So what's it about? My line of business or yours?"

"Yours."

Archer grinned appreciatively. Dressed in his "scruff," as he called it, a leather bomber jacket and jeans, dark hair cropped close to his skull, he wouldn't have looked out of place in a crowd of football hooligans or late Saturday night rowdies in the town centre. To Rudd's knowledge, he had been stopped and questioned several times by over-keen new beat men who hadn't recognised him.

"Go on," he said. "Surprise me."

"Do the names Lucy Blake and Jed Kemp mean anything to you?"

"They're not on my list. Why?"

"They've turned up in a murder investigation at Selhaven. They're on grass. I smelt it when I went to interview the girl. I didn't meet Kemp but he owns a boat," a small cabin cruiser, the "Lucy Fair," which he keeps moored on the river."

"Interesting," Archer commented. "Know anything else about them?"

"They were drinking at the Ring of Bells last night."

"Here in Chelmsford? That's a hell of a long way to come for a drink."

"That's what I thought. There may be nothing in it . . ."

"But it's worth a recce." Archer completed the sentence for him. "Got an address?"

Rudd wrote it down on a slip of paper, adding as he passed it across the table, "Kemp also runs a van—a green one."

"Muchos gracias," Archer said, folding up the paper and shoving it into the pocket of his jeans. "I'll get the boys on to it. Now come on, Jack, drink up. You owe me one, remember."

CHAPTER TEN

Promptly at five to ten the following morning, Rudd drove the short distance from the Kershaw museum to collect Nina Gifford at the King's Head Hotel, leaving Boyce in charge of the investigation; largely routine, at this stage. The major part of the search of the downstairs rooms was complete, and the main exhibits had been bagged up and sent off for forensic examination. All that remained was a search of the upper floor and the setting up of house-to-house inquiries in the neighbourhood, which he left Boyce to organise.

To Rudd's relief, Boyce, whose nosiness could be exasperating at times, had accepted without question the Chief Inspector's excuse that he needed to take a more detailed statement from Nina Gifford, together with a description of the Palmer drawing. Absurd though it was—for Boyce's attitude shouldn't have mattered a damn—Rudd felt his own conscience eased by Boyce's ready acceptance that the meeting was to be part of the investigation rather than a personal rendezvous.

She was waiting for him on the steps of the hotel, wearing the same skirt and jacket as she had the previous day and clutching an umbrella, even though the weather was warm—an encumbrance which she remarked on as she settled herself into the passenger seat beside him.

"God knows why I've brought the damned thing."

"Chuck it on the back seat," Rudd suggested.

As she did so, she gave him a brief smile, grateful and yet oddly tentative. It occurred to Rudd that, pleased though she was at this opportunity to visit Althorpe House, she regarded the trip with mixed feelings. It was, after all, where Max Gifford had died.

To take her mind off it, he said, "Tell me, what've you been doing with yourself recently?"

She said, "I'm living in London now, near Swiss Cottage. I bought the lease of a flat which I share with Danny."

It figured, Rudd thought, having met her brother during the Quinn murder investigation. The Chief Inspector had summed him up then as one of life's losers, adept at scrounging off anyone—usually women like Nina, who were fool enough to go on helping him out.

"How is your brother?" he asked, trying to sound genuinely interested. He heard in her voice the same note of false animation as she said, "Oh, he's fine. He's in Birmingham at the moment, looking for a job. That's why I was able to come down to Selhaven for a few days."

So Danny was out of work again, Rudd surmised, reading between the lines of Nina's reply. And evidently still expecting his sister to look after him. Nothing in that particular relationship appeared to have changed.

"And Althorpe House?" he went on. "I assume you sold that?"

"Yes, to someone who was going to turn it into a private nursing-home. I haven't been in touch with the new owner but I suppose it'll be all right for me to look round." She paused for a moment, and then said with that directness which he remembered had characterised her, "After Max killed himself, I didn't want to go on living there. There were too many memories. But it's the only place left that's got any connection with him. His old studio in London was pulled down years ago to make way for a supermarket. I just wanted to remind myself of what the house was like. Silly, I suppose, but there you are."

"Understandable," Rudd murmured in reply.

He guessed she was lonely, and that the visit to Althorpe was intended to be more than a mere return to the house where she and Max had once lived. It was also an attempt to recapture some of the lost happiness of that period in her life—a desire he could understand from his own relationship with Marion—although he doubted if it were wise. The past was a dangerous country. Once past its frontier, it was better not to look back.

He was struck, too, by the similarity between Nina's situation and Imogen Kershaw's. His own, as well. All of them had shared close bonds with a sibling, in their cases a brother, in his a sister; except his were now largely broken. It was a form of surrogate marriage, he supposed, which could be more binding than the relationship between a husband and wife. The recollections of a shared childhood could create powerful ties.

Nina was asking, "And what about you?"

He knew he would have to reciprocate by offering her some personal account, but he was conscious of keeping her at arm's length when he said, "I'm fine; busy, of course. Crime seems to be one of the growth industries." And then, to change the subject, although he needed the information, he added, "Tell me, when you saw Mr. Porlock at the museum, was anything said either by him or Miss Kershaw to suggest he intended going back there later to speak to her privately?"

"No, nothing."

"Or by Lucy Blake?"

"No but I saw her for only a few minutes. I have remembered something else though, since I spoke to you yesterday. Just as I was leaving the museum in the morning after I'd looked round it, there was a man coming up to the front door—Clive somebody or other. Miss Kershaw seemed pleased to see him. He said something about not being able to stay long; he'd called in on his way to catch the train."

She must be referring to Clive Osborne, Rudd thought. The name fitted, and Ambrose Scott, in the course of his statement, had mentioned that Osborne had been in London for the day. He had returned Scott's phone call after he'd got back to Selhaven.

Although he had yet to interview Osborne, this latest piece of evidence from Nina might be useful in corroborating Osborne's movements on the day Imogen Kershaw was murdered.

More out of curiosity and the desire to keep the conversation going on this less personal level than concern over Nina's opinion, he asked, "What was he like?" and was surprised by the warmth of her reply.

"Oh, very good-looking. You could imagine him being quite an Adonis as a young man; what Max used to call one of the golden lads."

It was said with genuine admiration which also contained an amused indulgence at that type of masculine beauty which certainly Max Gifford hadn't possessed himself, but which, as an artist, he had probably appreciated,—as evidently Nina did, too. Which was cheering. Rudd liked to think that Nina hadn't lost that sensual warmth which he had found so disturbing when he first met her.

He glanced at her obliquely.

She was sitting very upright in the passenger seat beside him, rather like, he thought, although the comparison was ridiculous, a little girl being taken out for a treat—her hands clasped in her lap, and her head constantly turning from side to side as she observed the details of the passing landscape, anxious to miss nothing. Each time her head moved, her ear-rings, long gold drops, swung against her cheeks and gave a touch of that Romany flamboyance to her appearance, which he remembered had been more pronounced during Max Gifford's lifetime.

Nina was aware of his covert glances and found them oddly embarrassing. When she was younger and Max had been alive, she had known how to deal with other men's admiration, finding it flattering and something of a game, an amusement which Max had shared.

"He fancies you," he'd say about some male friend or acquaintance, giving one of his great gusts of laughter. "And why not? You make a lovely lay."

It had added piquancy to their own love-making. But since Max's death, all the fun had gone out of it. She had grown more cautious, afraid that, now she was alone, she might be signalling her availability without being aware of doing so.

What was that saying? A woman is never more accessible than on the night after her husband dies. A bit of an exaggeration, but there was some truth in it all the same.

She was unsure also of quite how to deal with the Chief Inspector. Most men sent out signals which you didn't have to be all that clever to pick up. Rudd's were camouflaged. She guessed his loneliness but was uncertain how far he wanted to preserve it. He reminded her of those ordinary brown birds, like the thrushes, which she and Max had seen busy about the garden at Althorpe, inconspicuous and yet alert and lively, whose private lives, concealed among the leaves, were totally unknown.

They were approaching Althorpe, and Rudd slowed down to allow her more time to look about her. The village itself was unremarkable—a collection of houses and cottages, none of them picturesque, and some of them—such as the little close of new bungalows—positively ugly. There was a flint church, a shop, a garage, and a three-gabled village school. The stone lintels above the doors were still carved with the words "BOYS," "GIRLS" and "INFANTS," and its red brick walls were pitted with little round holes where earlier generations of children had ground their slate-pencils to points. There probably wasn't a Victorian school-building in England which didn't carry the same marks. His own had, Rudd remembered.

He couldn't gauge Nina's reactions. She kept her head turned away towards the passenger window; on purpose, he suspected. Even when they drove past Lionel Burnett's house, she made no sign that she had recognised it; poor old Lionel, whom Rudd had suspected of murdering Quinn out of jealousy of Nina whom Burnett himself had loved with such a deep and hopeless passion.

He must have survived, though. His front garden was as spruce as ever. A basket full of ivy-leaved geraniums hung over the front door, and a Ford Cortina, almost certainly his, was parked on the asphalted drive-in.

Rudd was tempted to make some reference to Burnett but there was no time. Even though he had dropped his speed down to twenty, they were approaching Althorpe House. Ahead of him, he could see the trees with their untidy clumps of rooks' nests, which marked the boundary of the grounds.

Flicking on the indicator for a left turn, he braked and changed down in readiness to draw into the entrance to the house.

Neither he nor Nina were prepared for what they saw. The drive and the tall, untidy hedge which had separated the garden from the road were there, but the five-barred gate which had once closed off the gap had been replaced by a high mesh grille, padlocked against intruders and bearing the sign of a demolition company.

Behind it, the drive, deeply rutted by the wheels of lorries, led to a space between the trees where Althorpe House had once stood, which was occupied now by nothing more than piles of brick rubble and scattered beams of wood.

Rudd was about to drive on, but before he could get the car into gear, Nina had opened the passenger door and was out and running along the verge. She ran awkwardly, like a woman trying to catch a bus, her handbag bumping on her arm and one hand clutching the edges of her jacket together. She must have discovered a gap in the hedge for, a moment later, Rudd saw her disappear between the bushes.

He followed her slowly, first locking up the car and then going to stand in front of the mesh gates, his hands stuffed deep in his pockets as he contemplated what remained of the house, before tramping off up the road in the direction Nina had taken.

He found the gap twenty-five yards further on. Scrambling through it, he emerged into a shrubbery which he remembered had formed part of the garden. At the edge of it, he paused again. There was no sign of Nina, but from this closer vantage point, it was possible to pick out certain features of what had been Althorpe House. The two steps which had led up to the front door were still there, and over to the right was the cobbled area which formerly had been the kitchen yard. A range of out-buildings had once stood facing it, and it was in one of these that Quinn's body had been found.

Of the rest of it—the warm, untidy kitchen where he had interviewed Nina, the big conservatory which had been Max Gifford's studio, the dining-room where his canvases had been stacked against the walls—nothing remained, although parts of the garden had been spared. Behind the demolition site, he could see the orchard. Some of the apple trees were still bearing like bright Christmas decorations, the small yellow fruits of this year's crop among the thinning foliage while, over to his left, the cedar tree stood like a dark, brooding presence.

Nina was standing beside it, her grey jacket showing up as a pale shape against its trunk.

Rudd walked towards her, skirting the rubble and the black circles in the grass where the waste lumber had been burned. He came to a halt on the far side of the site where the conservatory had once stood, judging by the shards of broken glass and the patches of coloured tiles set in the ground which had formed its floor.

Nina was leaning against the tree, as if drawing strength from it, her hands pressed to its bark and her back towards him.

It was impossible to tell if she was weeping, she stood so motionless. Rudd himself stood as quietly, waiting.

She turned at last, saw him, and made an effort to recover, bundling her hair back with one hand, the other scrubbing her handkerchief across her eyes with a curiously harsh movement before she began walking towards him. As she came closer, Rudd could see that her face was still streaked with tears, dirty with the dust from the bark.

"I'm sorry," he said. He meant it to encompass everything; her distress, the past, Max's death, the destruction which lay all about them and, finally, his own inadequacy.

"It can't be helped," Nina said, sniffing and smiling at the same time. "I was a fool to come. It's always a mistake to go back. And Max isn't here anyway. I should have known that, too. Even the summer-house has gone."

She gestured across the garden to where it had once stood amongst the trees, facing the overgrown tennis court. The whole area had been bulldozed flat.

Rudd said, "I'll drive you back to Selhaven."

He could think of nothing else to add which wouldn't have sounded trite; no words of comfort, no philosophical observation which might have had something positive to say about life's mutability, or death's inevitability.

He even hesitated to offer her his arm, in case the action implied an intimacy which she might not, under the circumstances, wish to receive.

All he could do for her, once they had returned to the car, was to leave her alone for a few moments to repair her make-up. When at last he climbed into the driver's seat beside her, the interior smelt faintly sweet with the scent of her powder.

For about half a minute she was silent, and then as they drove past the Feathers public house on the outskirts of the village, she remarked suddenly, "Max and I used to drink there before he got too crippled with arthritis to walk far."

"Do you want me to stop?" Rudd asked.

"Not there; somewhere else," Nina replied. "I could do with a brandy."

He bought her one at the next pub they came to, together with half a pint of bitter for himself. He carried the drinks over to the hearth at the far end of the bar, where a small logfire was burning, and where Nina was standing, holding out each foot in turn towards its warmth.

She had put on too much lipstick and her mouth looked too bright and stretched as she smiled and took the glass from him.

"It's nice here," she remarked, nodding round at the low-ceilinged room, the red flowered curtains and the bar counter, where a potted chrysanthemum was standing next to the beer handles. "Cosy. Max would have liked it." And then, without any further preamble, she asked, "Have you ever been in love?"

It would have been easy enough to shrug off the question. Instead, Rudd heard himself saying, "Once."

"Badly?"

"Bad enough."

"Like me and Max?"

"I think so. It's difficult to say."

He meant it was impossible to measure.

"Yes," she agreed, adding with a little laugh, "Why do we always say *badly* in love? I've never understood. Why not wonderfully? Or magically?"

"Or crazily?" Rudd suggested involuntarily, thinking of his own feelings for Marion Greave.

"There's that, too," Nina replied. "Like I was with Max. There's usually one, isn't there, who's more in love than the other?"

She was looking down into her glass as she spoke, not at him, although Rudd realised that she was referring not just to her relationship with Max—and perhaps also with Danny—but to his with Marion Greave. Even though he had said little about it, it had been enough for her to guess its nature.

He said awkwardly, feeling suddenly vulnerable, "I think we ought to be going."

She took the hint. Finishing up her brandy, she followed him out to the car.

Nothing more was said on the subject during the drive back to Selhaven. The conversation turned instead to Nina's written statement and the need for her to give a full description of the missing Palmer drawing at the incident room, which had been set up at the local police station.

He escorted her inside the building where, before handing her over to the uniformed Sergeant who would take down the written details, he made sure of her arrangements for getting back to London.

Did she need a lift to the station?

"No, I'll manage," she told him. "I've only got the one case and it isn't heavy. I've left it at the hotel reception."

They were standing in the entrance lobby among the plastic chairs and the posters pinned up on the notice-boards. It was not the place he would have chosen in which to say goodbye to her, a disadvantage which Nina herself seemed aware of, for she seemed unsure whether or not to shake hands.

In the end, they did, their hands meeting briefly and then parting.

"Thanks for the lift," she said.

He smiled, adding at the moment when she turned away, "Take care."

The next instant, the duty officer had released the security lock and she had disappeared through the door towards the interview rooms. The uniformed bulk of the Sergeant accompanying her cut off Rudd's view of any further sight of her.

He was about to leave and had started to walk towards the outer doors when he heard his name called.

Inspector Bayliss was signalling to him from behind the desk.

"I'm glad I've caught you, Chief Inspector," he remarked. When he and Rudd were installed inside Bayliss's first-floor office, he said, "It's about Mr. Scott. Fowles, one of the beat men, has reported seeing him coming out of Miss Kershaw's front gate late Wednesday evening."

"What time was this?" Rudd asked sharply.

"At quarter past eleven."

"And he's quite sure it was Scott?"

"Absolutely. He was one of the PCs sent on a house-to-house last year about a series of break-ins in Scott's road. Fowles had interviewed him then, and he was positive it was Scott he saw on Wednesday night. There's a street lamp not far from the gate and he was able to get a good look at him." He leaned across the desk to pass a sheet of paper to the Chief Inspector. "Fowles has typed out a report. It's all down there if you want to read it."

Rudd glanced down the page quickly. The statement was expressed in the dead pan official language which—while it could raise an amused eyebrow among the barristers in court, especially when read aloud in a halting manner by an inexperienced police witness—at least had the merit of presenting the facts briefly and cogently.

It began:

"At 23:15 on Wednesday, October 14th, while patrolling my beat along the south side of Church Crescent, I noticed a man emerging from the front garden gate of number 19, otherwise known as the William Kershaw Museum. . . ."

The report went on to state that as the man, Ambrose Scott, was known to PC Fowles as a respectable resident, he, Fowles, had not checked the premises but had continued his patrol, although he had noticed no lights were showing in the front windows of the house.

He had seen nothing else suspicious during his tour of the area.

"I'll keep this," Rudd said, folding up the sheet of paper and putting it away in his pocket. "You've got a copy, I assume, for your own files?" When Bayliss assured him that he had, Rudd continued, "I'd like a chat sometime with Fowles. I'll let you know when. In the meantime, could you arrange for a car to be sent round to Scott's house to pick him up at about three o'clock this afternoon? I shall need him to check on what's been stolen from the museum. At the same time, I can find out from him why the hell he said nothing to me yesterday about calling on Miss Kershaw the night she was murdered."

There was no sign of Nina when Rudd returned downstairs to the foyer, only the duty officer busy talking on the phone. Giving a brief nod in his direction, Rudd let himself out through the swing doors.

CHAPTER ELEVEN

Ambrose Scott arrived shortly after three o'clock, driven up to the gate in an unmarked police car and escorted to the door by a plain-clothes DC.

He looked, Rudd thought as he met him in the hall, taller and more gawky than before in a long black overcoat, a relic perhaps of his Civil Service days, and worn no doubt as a form of mourning. It gave him the appearance of an emaciated raven.

They began the tour in the museum itself, Boyce following behind them to note down any missing articles as Scott itemised them.

At first Scott seemed ill at ease, glancing nervously around him as if remembering the room as it had been on the morning he had discovered Imogen Kershaw's body. But it had been largely set to rights, the broken glass cleared away and the French windows sealed. The only signs that anything out of the ordinary had happened there were the aluminium powder still dusted across some of the surfaces, and the missing glass lid from the second cabinet, which had been unscrewed and taken away for forensic examination.

Scott concentrated on the contents of the display cabinets, calling out loud for Boyce's benefit those objects which were no longer on view.

The list was predictable and one which, by examining the labels, Rudd had already largely compiled for himself. It consisted of all the items of any value—William Kershaw's silver cigarette case, the gold watch and chain, a signet ring and a small silver and enamel snuff-box in which Kershaw used to carry saccharine tablets. And his penknife.

"Penknife?" Rudd repeated. It was an object which he had missed, and its theft seemed incongruous. "Was it valuable?"

"I don't think so," Scott said. "It was just an ordinary steel pocketknife. William used it for almost anything—cutting up fruit, sharpening pencils; that sort of thing. I can't think why anyone would want to take it."

Rudd let it pass. Any discussion of the purpose behind its theft was not for Scott's ears, although the Chief Inspector had his own theory. It had been used, he suspected, to prise open the French windows, yet another piece of evidence to support his theory that the burglary was a fake, carried out after Miss Kershaw was killed, and by someone who hadn't gone to the house prepared either to break into the house or to murder her. An unpremeditated killing, in other words.

"Is anything else missing?" he asked.

Scott peered uncertainly about the room.

"There was a photograph on the desk," he said at last. "An enlarged snapshot of the three of us, William, Clive and myself, punting on the backs at Cambridge. That's gone. It was in a silver frame; probably why it was stolen. I can't see that anything else has been taken."

There was nothing for it except to draw his attention to the blank space on the wall where the Palmer drawing had once hung.

"Oh, that; yes," Scott remarked, acknowledging its absence but apparently not impressed by its loss. "It was given to William by his grandfather. Evidently it'd been in the family for years and William had always liked it."

It appeared Scott had nothing more to add to the list, and they moved across the hall to Miss Kershaw's sitting-room which Scott refused to enter, remaining stubbornly on the threshold and repeating, "I don't think anything's gone from here. I really can't tell you."

It was pointless trying to force him. Eyes squeezed almost shut, Scott was turning his head this way and that, like a blind man straining to see. With a quick glance at Boyce, Rudd closed the door and led the way upstairs to the manuscript room.

"I believe you said that it was Miss Kershaw's habit to work up here most evenings on her brother's papers," Rudd remarked as they entered the room. "What exactly would she do?"

Scott himself seemed uncertain.

"Typing, I suppose. Or filing William's papers. I'm afraid he was rather a magpie. He kept everything—postcards, receipts, newspaper cuttings that happened to interest him."

"Quite a job coping with it all," Rudd remarked. "Careful, was she, about keeping everything in order?"

"Meticulous," Scott assured him.

"Just have a look over here," Rudd went on, waving an arm towards the shelf where the files of memorabilia were stored. "Notice anything?"

Scott went across the room, bending his awkward frame to peer at the labels. It was impossible to read his expression, but his profile, with its beaky nose, had a closed, secretive look about it. He stood for several seconds without speaking, shoulders hunched, as the Chief Inspector and the Sergeant waited for his reply.

"Well?" Rudd asked at last, exasperated by the man's silence.

Scott turned to face him.

"I don't see anything wrong, Chief Inspector. They're just files of, I imagine, personal bits and pieces which wouldn't fit into any other category; nothing of any great importance to William's literary life. Is that all?"

In the face of Scott's lack of response, there was nothing Rudd could do except press on with the rest of the interview.

"Just a couple more points. A pair of leather gloves, marked with the initials W. K., has been found. I assume they belonged to William Kershaw. Do you know whereabouts in the house they might have been kept?"

"They sound like the ones which were left on the edge of the brass container in the hall with the walking-sticks. William always left a pair there. If they're missing, then they're almost certainly the same. What was the other point? You said there were two."

"The other concerns the statement you made yesterday, Mr. Scott," Rudd said. "You told us that, after Mr. Osborne phoned you, you went straight to bed. But you were seen coming out of the front gate of the museum at a quarter past eleven."

"Ah!" Scott said. He was silent for a few moments, gazing down at his feet, planted on the worn carpet. Then he asked, "I suppose whoever it was reported seeing me?"

"Why didn't you mention it yourself?"

"Fear mainly, Chief Inspector; a cowardly sense of self-preservation. After all, I'd quarrelled with Imogen earlier in the day. In your eyes, I could have had a motive for murdering her. But it was also embarrassment. I didn't like to admit I'd been so concerned about her. It's women who are supposed to be intuitive, isn't it? Even after Clive rang me and told me to let the matter rest for the time being, I still felt that something was wrong. I can't put it any clearer than that. Anyway, I couldn't settle so I decided to walk round there."

"Intending what?"

Scott hoisted his bony shoulders.

"God knows. I'm not even sure myself. If there had been a light on, I might have rung the bell. But as there wasn't, I simply went home." His expression sombre, he turned to look at the Chief Inspector. "That's another reason why I didn't say anything to you. Guilt. I keep thinking if only I'd gone round to the back of the house, I'd've seen the house had been broken into and I might have been able to save her."

"But we only have his word for that," Rudd commented later to Boyce when, having dropped Scott off by car at the police station to make a written statement and to have his fingerprints taken, he and the Sergeant drove on to Osborne's house. "Supposing Miss Kershaw was still alive when Scott called and she let him in? He had the opportunity. The means were at hand— Kershaw's walking stick—and who'd know better than Scott where to find the murder weapon as well as the gloves? And I'm damned sure he noticed those files were out of order. If he's as innocent as he makes out, why didn't he mention it? As for motive—well, he's admitted he'd quarrelled with her over her scheme to republish her brother's books."

"Hardly a reason for bashing her over the head," Boyce objected.

"That may only be the half of it," Rudd said enigmatically.

The car had drawn up in the driveway of a large, detached house in a prosperous part of Selhaven, and there was no time to expand on the remark. As he got out, however, he was thinking that if he were right and Scott had been in love with Imogen Kershaw, it wouldn't have taken much to tip him over the edge. Years of frustration was a hell of a burden for any man to carry. One casual, unthinking remark on Imogen Kershaw's part could have been enough.

But where was the proof?

Slamming the passenger door behind him, he stood for a few seconds in Osborne's drive, looking about him.

Even before he met the man, his first impression of Clive Osborne was wealth; old, established money which was spent discreetly and with taste. There was nothing flashy about the dark grey BMW parked by the front door, nor about the house itself. It was pukka Georgian; its flat stucco facade, long sash windows and plain pillared porch expressed that understated elegance of style that needed no further embellishment in the way of brass carriage lamps or fancy shutters.

But it was the car which seemed to impress Boyce. He had stopped to examine it, bending down to look in at the pearl-grey upholstery and the twin stereo speakers, even running a hand across the bonnet, as if, Rudd thought as he waited for him in the porch, it were a woman he was caressing, although he doubted if Mrs. Boyce ever came in for such attention.

Even so, all the Sergeant felt the need to say, as he came up the steps to join Rudd, was, "Nice job, that," his own piece of understatement.

A grey-haired, middle-aged woman, Osborne's housekeeper,

Rudd assumed, opened the door to them and showed them across the hall and into a drawing-room where Osborne was waiting for them.

Entering it, Rudd was reminded of the illustrations in the back copies of the house and garden magazines which he sometimes glanced at in his dentist's waiting-room. The same adjectives used in the accompanying articles rose to mind—"graceful," "elegant," "tasteful."

Osborne's drawing-room was certainly all these. It was a large, pale room, furnished with chairs and sofas covered in glazed, pastel chintz, and the type of antique pieces which Wallingford would have favoured with their own individual spotlights. A collection of silver-framed photographs, without which no such setting seemed complete, was displayed on a long sofa table next to a bowl of roses. There were none of William Kershaw or his sister, Rudd noticed as he crossed the room; several of Osborne and his wife, though, in evening dress at various social functions, suggesting that they had occupied a position of some standing in Selhaven. Osborne's wife had a cool, disdainful look about her, bearing out Scott's description of her as something of a snob.

Osborne came forward to meet them, and as Rudd shook hands with him and introduced Boyce, the thought crossed the Chief Inspector's mind that the same epithets which could be used to describe the room were applicable to Osborne himself.

He, too, was elegant and tasteful, in the type of deceptively casual clothes—a pale blue cashmere sweater and grey trousers—which only those with taste and money themselves recognise as being not only exquisitely tailored but also extremely expensive. His manner had the same low-keyed charm; there was nothing flashy about that either.

As for his features, Rudd could understand Nina's remark that as a young man, he must have been one of the golden lads. He still preserved some of those fair, finely cut good looks which, when he was in his twenties, must have been spectacular.

Clive Osborne invited them to sit down. He was expecting them, as Rudd had taken the precaution of telephoning to arrange the interview. Rudd chose a chair facing the windows, through which he had a view of the garden, with its sweep of lawn and carefully tended rose-beds.

As he had done with Ambrose Scott, he began the interview in a general manner, establishing the background of Osborne's relationship with the Kershaws, brother and sister, a little of which he had already learned from Scott, and the details of which Osborne confirmed.

He had, he agreed, known the Kershaws since just before the war, having met William Kershaw while they were both under-graduates at Cambridge. Like Scott, he had maintained the friendship, visiting William and his sister first at Highgate and then, during the war, spending part of his army leaves at their cottage in Tolstead and later, after he was demobbed, at the house in Church Crescent.

"What was William Kershaw like?" Rudd asked.

He had made his own judgement of the man, which had been largely backed up by Scott. It would be interesting to hear Osborne's opinion, especially in view of the later estrangement between the two men.

Osborne's reply surprised him.

"He was enormously good fun to be with," he said.

"Was he?" Rudd said. It was a new and unexpected impression of William Kershaw. "In what way?"

"He could be very amusing; he enjoyed life. It was a pity he didn't express that side of himself in his books. He tended to take his writing too seriously. As he grew older, he lost a lot of that sense of fun and became more and more difficult and eccentric. I think he was bitter that he hadn't been recognised as a first-rate writer. He minded about that very much. You know, do you, that he and I broke off the friendship after my marriage?"

"Tell me about it," Rudd said, committing himself neither to confirming nor denying the question.

"It was unfortunate," Osborne replied, a note of genuine regret in his voice, "but I suppose, looking back on it, we simply grew apart."

And that was that. He said nothing more about Kershaw's dislike of his new rich friends; nothing either about Mrs. Osborne's antipathy towards the relationship. His reluctance to discuss his personal affairs, Rudd supposed, was understandable under the circumstances, and left him with no alternative except to move on to the next part of the interview.

"I believe you helped manage Miss Kershaw's affairs after the death of her brother?"

"I suppose Ambrose told you that?" Osborne said more sharply. "Is it relevant?"

There was an impatience in his voice which, like Osborne's remarks about Kershaw, took the Chief Inspector by surprise. It was not a reaction he had been expecting.

He said in a conciliatory voice, "Only as a general background to Miss Kershaw's murder."

"But wasn't it the result of a burglary? Ambrose rang and told me it was. Someone broke into the museum and Imogen must have disturbed him. I can't see that her finances have anything to do with it. Her death was enough of a shock without having her private affairs pried into."

"Yes, I see," Rudd said, appearing to agree although he couldn't make the connection between the shock of Miss Kershaw's murder and the state of her finances. Was Osborne implying that the same emotional stress applied to both? If so, why? Or was Osborne merely trying to convey that he still felt too distressed by her death to consider explaining her accounts to him, especially as he regarded such an inquiry irrelevant in the first place?

It was better, Rudd decided, to leave it there. If Imogen Kershaw's financial position ever became significant, such as the question of who would benefit under her will, he could always go back to Osborne and press him for details.

"I'd like to move on to Wednesday, the day Miss Kershaw was murdered. Did you see her at any time?" he asked, as if he knew nothing of Osborne's visit to the museum that morning.

"Yes, as a matter of fact, I called on her briefly on the way to the station. There was only time for Imogen to tell me that she was hoping to arrange for the re-publication of William's novels."

"Did you approve?"

"Approve, Chief Inspector?" Osborne seemed taken aback by the word. "There wasn't the opportunity to discuss the idea in detail. Imogen merely explained her scheme to me."

Rudd found the answer as unsatisfactory in its way as Osborne's surroundings. It was too bland, too non-commital, especially when compared with the warmth of Scott's reaction to Imogen Kershaw's plan. Perversely, he wanted to stir Osborne up into something of the same emotional response.

He said deliberately, "Mr. Scott disagreed. I gather he quarrelled with Miss Kershaw over her plans to republish."

"Yes, I realise that. I spoke to Ambrose later that evening on the phone and he told me about it."

"Why should he react so strongly? Have you any idea?"

"I think you should ask him that."

"I'm asking you."

There was a small silence in which Rudd sensed not only Osborne's disapprobation, but Boyce's as well. He was aware that he was handling this part of the interview badly, but could not quite understand why it had slipped out of his control, or how he could retrieve it.

It was Osborne who saved the situation with that ease of charm and good manners, which had no doubt seen him safely through other social difficulties.

He said, "I think Ambrose was concerned that Imogen would be disappointed. There was very little chance that any publisher would be interested in re-issuing William's books and, once she went into the costs of publishing privately, she'd realise they were beyond her means. Although she could be stubborn, she also had a lot of common sense. Given time, she'd realise that the idea was impractical."

"And you thought this was the best way to handle the situation?"

"Under the circumstances, yes. I told Ambrose so."

They seemed to have reached the end of that particular line of inquiry and Rudd changed tack.

"Several items were taken from the museum. Have you any idea if Miss Kershaw kept anything of real value in the house?"

"Not to my knowledge."

"What about the Palmer drawing?"

Osborne looked puzzled.

"What Palmer drawing?"

"A small sketch of a woodland scene which was hanging to the left of the fireplace."

"Was that a Palmer? In that case, it would have been worth quite a lot of money. Imogen always said it was but she tended to overestimate the value of anything that belonged to William."

The minor issues had been dealt with, and Rudd continued, getting to the heart of the interview, "To return to the day of the Miss Kershaw's murder, we'll need a statement of your movements."

"Of course, Chief Inspector," Osborne replied with a return to his courteous manner. "Would you prefer I wrote it down? It will save your Sergeant making notes."

When Rudd nodded his assent, Osborne got up from his chair with the grace of a much younger man, and, moving across the room to a small rosewood desk, sat down and began to write.

Behind his back, Boyce exchanged a glance with Rudd that expressed a complexity of emotions—surprise at the Chief Inspector's abrupt attitude to Osborne and a rueful acknowledgement of the man's good manners in dealing with it. It was fair comment, and Rudd raised one shoulder in response, admitting both.

Osborne was several minutes in completing his statement. When he returned with it and handed it to the Chief Inspector, Rudd glanced at it quickly before passing it over to Boyce. It was a neatly drawn-up schedule, listing Osborne's appointments in London on the day of Miss Kershaw's murder. He had, it appeared, spent a full day, which had included visits to his barber and his tailor, lunch at Fortnum and Mason's and dinner at his club, the Varsity, in Wardle Street. It was the last part of the statement that covered the evening which drew Rudd's attention.

"I see you caught the 9:25 from Liverpool Street," he remarked.

"Yes, that's right. Unfortunately, I just missed the earlier train, the 8:10, by a few minutes. I dined early at my club, fully intending to catch it but my taxi got held up in traffic. It was annoying as it meant waiting on Liverpool Street station for over an hour. Not all the trains stop at Selhaven."

"Did you meet anyone you knew?"

"On the station? No, I didn't; nor on the train. But the ticket collector at Selhaven may remember me."

"What time did you get back to the house?"

"I suppose about quarter to eleven. It takes about ten minutes to walk from the station. I rarely bother to take the car. I enjoy the exercise. My housekeeper may remember the time I arrived. She was still up when I got in."

"I understand you rang Mr. Scott soon afterwards?"

"Yes; almost immediately. He'd rang earlier that evening and left a message that I was to phone him back. He was concerned about an argument he'd had with Imogen about her plan to republish William's books. It was then that I advised him to let the matter drop. After that I had supper and went to bed."

"You didn't leave the house again later that evening?"

"No, Chief Inspector, I did not," Osborne said, still courteous but with a harder edge to his voice, which drew no response from the Chief Inspector, except for a non-committal, "Yes, I see, sir," although he followed it up almost immediately with the comment, "We'll need a written statement from you, Mr. Osborne, and you'll have to have your fingerprints taken."

It was Boyce who softened the remark by adding, "It's for elimination purposes, Mr. Osborne."

"Yes, I quite understand," Osborne said politely.

"May I speak to your housekeeper?" Rudd put in, ignoring both Boyce and his comment.

"Of course," Osborne replied without any hesitation. "I'll fetch her."

He left the room, returning shortly with the middle-aged, grey-haired woman who had opened the door to them. Having introduced her as Mrs. Wharton, Osborne remarked, "I'll leave you alone to speak to her," and went out again, closing the door behind him.

"Sit down, Mrs. Wharton," Rudd told her. "This won't take long."

She perched herself nervously on the edge of one of the armchairs, unused, it seemed, to being invited to sit in Osborne's drawing-room. She answered Rudd's questions willingly, and as the interview progressed, even relaxed far enough to expand on some of her replies.

To set her at her ease, Rudd began with more general questions regarding her role in the household, before moving on to the events of the day of Imogen Kershaw's murder.

"I believe Mr. Osborne was in London on Wednesday? What time did he get back?"

"At quarter to eleven, off the 10:35 train. He said he'd just missed the earlier one which gets in at twenty past nine."

"You're sure about the time?"

"Oh, quite sure. I'd expected him off the 8:10 from London, the one he usually catches. When he didn't arrive, I kept an eye on the clock, guessing he'd be on the next. I always leave out sandwiches for him, you see, and I wanted to make sure I took them out of the fridge in good time and heated up the coffee percolator. He was home, as I said, by quarter to eleven. It takes him about ten minutes to walk from the station."

"I believe he phoned Mr. Scott soon after he got in?"

"That's right, sir. Mr. Scott had rung earlier and asked me to tell Mr. Osborne to phone him back when he got home. I passed on the message and Mr. Osborne rang him straight away, almost as soon as he got inside the door."

"You didn't happen to overhear any of the conversation?"

"Only Mr. Osborne asking Mr. Scott what he wanted. I was on my way upstairs to hang Mr. Osborne's overcoat up to dry."

"Did he go out again that evening?"

"Not to my knowledge, sir. He said goodnight to me at about quarter past eleven. I cleared away the supper things, locked up and then went to bed myself. I'm sure I'd've heard him if he left the house."

"But she could have been mistaken," Rudd remarked as he and Boyce left the house.

"What's up with you?" Boyce demanded. "Anybody'd think you wanted to find Osborne guilty."

Rudd stood for a few moments in the drive, hands stuffed deep in his pockets as he looked back at Osborne's house, the semi-circular rose-beds on either side of the porch, and the gleaming BMW.

"It's not that, Tom," he remarked, climbing into the car at last and slamming the passenger door shut. "There's something about the man that . . ."

He left it there, unable to find the words to express his antipathy, not so much towards Osborne himself, but for a lifestyle which seemed too easy, too unchallenging. He wanted to find some flaw in it, a small sign of canker in the flower, but could discover nothing.

Instead, he continued, "We'll get Kyle to check his alibi tomorrow morning, especially the time of the train Osborne got off at Selhaven. And while we're in the car, drive round to the station. I'd like to get some idea of the route he'd've taken and how long it'd take to walk it."

It was three minutes by car; ten minutes, at least, on foot, as Boyce pointed out as they drove into the station forecourt and out again.

"If he came off that 10:35 train, there's no way he'd've had the time to stop off at the museum, clobber Miss Kershaw over the head and fake that burglary. Besides, where's his motive? He seemed on good terms with Miss Kershaw, not like Scott. And why should either of them want to steal that drawing? Neither of them knew it was by Palmer."

It was Rudd who had the last word on that one.

"Why should any of them apart from Lucy Blake, Wallingford or Chadwick? Certainly not your average thief, Tom, who wouldn't know a Palmer from a stick of rhubarb. I think we'll make a little trip up to London ourselves tomorrow and have a chat with Chadwick, alias Mr. Porlock."

CHAPTER TWELVE

The following afternoon, Rudd and Boyce set off by train to London, to interview Maurice Chadwick by appointment, Rudd having telephoned to warn him of their arrival but prudently refusing to state the reason for their visit.

"I'd rather not discuss it on the phone, Mr. Chadwick," he said, assuming that official, deadpan voice which on occasions had its uses.

The trip was something of a diversion. It had been an unsatisfactory morning, taken up entirely by routine tasks which had come up with nothing of any use to the investigation. On the house-to-house inquiries—nil; no-one had heard or seen anything unusual on Wednesday evening.

Kyle's report on Osborne's alibi had yielded the same negative results. The man had spent the day, as he had stated, in London, returning to Selhaven on the 10:35 train. The ticket collector had remembered him handing in his ticket at the barrier.

"He's quite sure it was Osborne?" Rudd asked, looking for a chink of light.

"Positive," Kyle replied. "Osborne travels up to London fairly frequently. The man recognised him straight away."

"So that puts Osborne out of the running," Boyce remarked after Kyle had left the office. "His housekeeper said he was home by quarter to eleven. As it'd take him at least ten minutes to walk from the station, there's no way he had time to murder Miss Kershaw and fake the burglary. He'd need about half an hour for that. Besides, where's his motive?"

Which left Scott or Lucy Blake and her boy-friend. Or Chadwick, so far the outsider.

And not a scrap of hard evidence to pin on any of them, Rudd thought.

It was nix all round, as Boyce put it later when they were in the train on the way to London.

From Liverpool Street station, they caught the underground to Hyde Park, emerging up the steps into the soft brilliance of the late afternoon.

It might have been July. There were people strolling about in the park, where only the thinning foliage on the trees suggested that it was mid-October. The sky was paint-box blue, the sort of pure expanse of colour that children use to depict the immaculate, unclouded skies of high summer.

The flowers, still blooming in the window-boxes and gardens of the hotels and blocks of mansion flats, might also have been painted in with little dabs of geranium-pink, mimula-yellow and that bright, almost fluorescent scarlet of salvias.

Maurice Chadwick's house, tucked away in a discreet side street behind Park Lane, had window-boxes. It also had neat, fitted awnings in broad white and blue stripes. It was stuccoed, with curly wrought-iron balconies and security-grilles over the windows; vaguely Moorish in style—it was a millionaire's villa, lifted bodily from some exotic, bougainvillaea-hung location in the Mediterranean, and set down among the more sedate brick and tile of Mayfair.

A Filippino manservant showed them into a large hall with several arched doorways, the tiled floor overlaid with Oriental rugs, and down several carpeted steps into an even larger drawing-room, where Maurice Chadwick was waiting to receive them.

He was a short, round man, out of proportion with the loftiness and grandeur of his surroundings. He had a shiny look about him, from the texture of his suit, softly moulded to his plump, little body, to his balding head where his hair had been brushed up over his ears into two gleaming cockades.

As they shook hands and Rudd introduced himself and Boyce,

Chadwick's smile flashed briefly at them—one, two—as if he were taking their photographs.

"Do sit down," he told them, waving them towards two low armchairs, covered in raw silk, the cushions of which sighed gently as they subsided into them.

It was a white room—white carpet, white furniture, white walls, the only colour supplied by Chadwick himself in his pale blue shirt and pink tie. And by the pictures which hung three deep on every side.

"Coffee?" Chadwick was saying.

As he busied himself with the silver coffee-pot, which the manservant had placed on a low table next to three tiny gold cups, Rudd glanced about him.

It was like looking at a series of oblong windows, each one opening onto a portion of English countryside. Here the Yorkshire moors swept away, heather-coloured, under a thunderous sky; there, the softer, rounded landscape of Suffolk, perhaps, lay gently at rest, alongside a view which might be of the Fens in winter, a study in white like the room itself.

He knew little about art but guessed he was examining a private collection which was probably worth a fortune. Nina could have told him. She would almost certainly have recognised at least some of the artists. Even to Rudd's untutored eye, the Suffolk scene had a look of Constable about it, in the vista of meadow and ploughland stretching back to a far-off church, and the misty curve of a river.

He was reminded also of the Kershaw museum, incongruous though that comparison might be. Yet it was not entirely invalid. Both collections, Chadwick's and Imogen Kershaw's, had an obsessive quality about them and it crossed his mind, as he leaned forward to take the tiny gold coffee cup from Chadwick, that between them, Chadwick and Miss Kershaw could constitute the perfect murderer and his victim: she was the possessor of something he so ardently desired—the Palmer drawing.

Chadwick had settled himself back into his chair, his little legs crossed, perfectly relaxed.

"I see you're admiring my water-colours, Chief Inspector," he remarked.

"It's a fine collection," Rudd replied.

"A lifetime's hobby. But what's money for, if not to be spent on beautiful objects?"

Rudd inclined his head but refrained from commenting that in his case, it was the mortgage and the gas bill which claimed priority.

The preliminary skirmish was over. He and Chadwick had circled round one another, taking each other's measure. It had been delicately carried out. Rudd only wished to God Boyce looked more at ease. He was sitting bolt upright against the white silk cushions in his best dark suit and a rather unfortunate tie—banded, like Chadwick's awnings, in broad blue and white stripes, the little gold cup held awkwardly in his great hands, as he peered suspiciously down at the strong, black Turkish brew, as if he suspected it would dissolve the gilding.

"And to what," Chadwick continued, "do I owe the pleasure of your visit, Chief Inspector?"

He probably had some idea that it was connected with his trip to Selhaven. The man was no fool, and it wouldn't take much intelligence to make the connection between the visit and a request for an interview from a senior CID officer based at Divisional Headquarters in Chelmsford.

Rudd said, "It's about the Kershaw museum, Mr. Chadwick. I believe you visited it on Wednesday morning?"

"How clever of you," Chadwick replied, flashing his smile again. "I wonder how you discovered that?"

"Where you showed some interest in a drawing on display there," Rudd continued, ignoring Chadwick's question.

"What particular drawing had you in mind? There were quite a few; most of them rather inept little sketches, as I remember, of no special artistic merit."

"I'm speaking of the Palmer," Rudd said.

"Ah," Chadwick replied and waited.

Rudd set down his coffee cup on the table as if he were laying down his cards.

"I'll be frank with you, Mr. Chadwick. I've spoken to Mr. Wallingford who's admitted his part in the proposed deal to buy the picture. I'd like to hear your side of the account, so that I'll know I've got the record perfectly straight."

He spoke with the sincere, slightly contrite tone of a man anxious to get at the truth. He had deliberately assumed the tone in order to put Chadwick on the defensive, and he was gratified when the man immediately bristled up.

"I have no idea what Wallingford's told you but I can assure you that the deal, as you call it, was perfectly legitimate. Wallingford rang me about a month ago to tell me that he'd located a drawing which could be by Palmer and which he thought I might be interested in. He suggested that I had a look at it and, if it were authentic and I wished to buy, he'd try to make arrangements to acquire it on my behalf through a third party."

"He didn't say who that person was?"

"No. I gathered, though, that it was someone friendly with the owner, a Miss Kershaw, who would be better placed to persuade her to sell than either Wallingford or myself."

Lucy Blake, in other words, Rudd thought. The description could apply to no-one else.

"So you went along to the Kershaw museum on Wednesday morning to check the picture out," Rudd continued, "and signed the visitors' book with a false name and address. Why did you bother to do that, Mr. Chadwick?"

"Isn't it obvious, Chief Inspector? If the deal went through, my name might have come up in connection with it. I preferred to remain incognito as far as my visit to the museum was concerned."

But it wasn't simply for that reason, Rudd suspected. From the jaunty look on Chadwick's face, he guessed that the man had enjoyed that cloak-and-dagger element in the negotiations, as well as the fun of choosing a pseudonym and deceiving Miss

Kershaw over his real identity. To him, it had been like taking part in an amusing schoolboy prank.

"And what exactly were the terms of the deal?" he asked.

"They hadn't been worked out in detail," Chadwick said snappishly, annoyed at being brought down to essentials. "Wallingford would obviously take a commission; so would whoever it was who'd arranged to buy the picture in the first place."

"And what about yourself, Mr. Chadwick?"

"I don't understand you," Chadwick retorted, his plump little mouth clamping shut like a child refusing to confess.

"I assume you weren't going to lose out on the deal," Rudd suggested.

"Well, of course not, Chief Inspector, although, once I'd seen the drawing, it was worth far more to me than any amount of cash you could name. It was an exquisite little sketch with a sepia wash; a perfect example of Palmer's later work."

His eyes glittered at the memory, as if he were speaking of a woman.

"The deal," Rudd reminded him.

Chadwick owned up at last.

"Wallingford would have sold it to me for slightly less than its market value; say, five hundred pounds off the agreed price. But, as I said, the terms had still to be negotiated."

"What might it have fetched?"

"At auction? Anything between two and four thousand, possibly more, depending on who else was bidding. I was prepared to go up to three."

So, supposing Miss Kershaw had agreed to part with it for two to three hundred and, allowing for a commission, say, of another couple of hundred for Lucy Blake, Wallingford stood to gain at least two thousand from the transaction, not a bad profit when, as far as Rudd could make out, he'd done nothing more to earn it than make a few phone calls.

Chadwick had evidently been doing his own calculations, putting two and two together and coming up with a serious discrepancy in Rudd's apparent motive for interviewing him. For he

suddenly said, "Just a moment, Chief Inspector. Why exactly
are you here? You and your Sergeant haven't come all the way
from Essex merely to inquire into the sale of one small drawing
which hasn't even changed hands yet."

It was time to come clean.

"The Kershaw museum was burgled on Wednesday
night . . ." Rudd began.

"Oh, my God!" Chadwick exclaimed. "The Palmer's been
stolen!"

". . . and Miss Kershaw was murdered."

"Oh, my God!" Chadwick repeated in exactly the same tone
with which he had anticipated the theft of the drawing.

Rudd glanced across at Boyce, inviting him to take over the
questioning, and sat back as he prepared to enjoy the next few
minutes. He guessed Boyce would take the opportunity to pay
Chadwick out for his disgusting coffee, his armchairs—too low
for the bulky Sergeant to sit in comfortably—and for making
him feel subtly disadvantaged, although Boyce would have hotly
denied the charge had the Chief Inspector taxed him with it.

It was interesting to see how the balance of power shifted
suddenly, Boyce coming into his own, Chadwick the one now
defending his corner, and not making a very good job of it.

Boyce said in his heavy, professional voice, "We'd like a statement of your movements on Wednesday, Mr. Chadwick."

"This is ridiculous!" Chadwick protested, bouncing up and
giving Rudd a look of appeal. But the Chief Inspector was gazing
across at the water-colours on the opposite wall, with an expression of approval which could have been intended simply for
them.

"Are you saying that you refuse to co-operate in our inquiries?" Boyce asked, exuding a faint aura of menace and adding
the word "sir" only after a perceptible pause.

At this point, Rudd intervened, the reasonable copper.

"I don't think we'll need a full statement from Mr. Chadwick,
Sergeant. After all, we know his movements for part of the day,
don't we? He was at the Kershaw museum in the morning and

visiting Mr. Wallingford's antique shop in the early part of the afternoon. Shall we pick up your account from the time you left Mr. Wallingford's?"

Defeated, Chadwick sighed and sank down into his chair, with much the same sound and movement that the cushions had made when sat on.

Speaking quickly, as if to get the ordeal over and done with as quickly as possible, he said, "I had tea in the King's Head Hotel. I then looked round a small junk shop in a side street—I don't know its name. As there was nothing there of any interest, I walked to the station and caught the 5:12 train from Selhaven which got into Liverpool Street at about twenty past six. From there, I got a taxi home. I dined alone, watched the news on television, read for an hour or so and went to bed at about eleven."

"Can anyone corroborate your statement? Your manservant, for example?"

"It was his night off. After he'd served dinner at seven o'clock, he went out to visit friends and wasn't back until after midnight."

"So you were alone for most of the evening?" Boyce asked, rubbing it in. "What about the ticket collector at Selhaven station? Would he remember you?"

"There was no-one on the barrier when I arrived. There was a clerk on duty at the ticket counter but I didn't speak to him and I don't think he noticed me. I'd already bought a return ticket in London so I simply went straight on to the platform. There were a few other people waiting for the train. One of them may have seen me."

"We'll have to check, won't we?" Boyce said, putting away his notebook. Both the tone and the gesture suggested that he didn't hold out much hope of Chadwick's alibi being substantiated.

A little later, the interview over, he and Rudd walked back along Park Lane towards the underground station. Surprisingly, Boyce remarked, "I can't see Chadwick doing it."

"Why not?" Rudd asked, playing devil's advocate. "He's got motive and opportunity."

"Opportunity, yes. I'll give you that," Boyce replied magnanimously. "If he was alone from seven o'clock onwards, he'd've had just about enough time to nip back to Selhaven on the train and call on Miss Kershaw, perhaps to put in his own bid for the drawing."

"He'd be cutting it fine," Rudd pointed out. "Scott phoned her at a quarter to ten and there was no answer. If we assume she was already dead by then . . ."

"She needn't have been. She could've simply ignored the phone, like Scott himself thought at the time. It's possible she was murdered later on Wednesday evening. In which case, Chadwick could have just about made it. It's the motive which doesn't add up. Would he want to murder someone simply for a drawing? I mean, I ask you. He's obviously not short of a bob or two. Look at that house of his, not to mention the bloody manservant. And what was the drawing worth anyway? A couple of thousand. Four at the most. That'd be peanuts to someone like Chadwick."

"It's not the value. Chadwick said that himself. It's the *possessing* that counts."

"Well, I for one don't get it," Boyce said heavily.

But Rudd understood. And it was not only the acquisition of the desired object which was important, although that was the ultimate prize. It was the negotiations which led up to it, the subtle manoeuvres, and the thrill, in the bidding and counter-bidding, of outwitting one's opponents.

It could become obsessional, a fever in the blood. He'd known some gamblers possess it. It was this that kept the stock-markets booming, as well as the racecourses, the roulette tables and the auction rooms.

He wasn't surprised at Boyce's inability to make the connection. The Sergeant was a man of few passions and almost no obsessions, except over the quality of draught bitter and the professional incompetence of any police officer above the rank of Superintendent.

But Max Gifford would have understood immediately and so, too, would Nina.

They had reached the steps leading down to the underground station where Rudd paused, his hand on the rail, to look back.

The park had blossomed with lights, glittering between the branches of the trees, while above them the sky had taken on a reddish bloom like plush. There was a complex odour in the air, compounded of exhaust fumes, damp earth and the rich fragrance of coffee from a nearby restaurant.

It was absurd to feel nostalgic when he wasn't sure exactly what it was he pined for. Not for London. Nor for the promise of pleasure which the hotels with their tiers of lighted windows held out for him, or for the couple who at that moment walked past him along the pavement, arms about each other, the woman laughing.

Boyce was saying with a generous air, "The fact Chadwick gave a false name and address is iffy. I'll grant you that. But I still think that drawing's not enough of a motive."

He had gone down a few steps, where he waited for the Chief Inspector to catch up with him, impatient at the delay. His face turned up to look back at Rudd, the hideous striped tie hanging loose outside his jacket.

"If we get a move on," he added, "we'll make the 6:52 from Liverpool Street."

Rudd came to a decision, so suddenly that it surprised even himself.

"If you don't mind, Tom," he said, coming down the steps, "I won't come back with you to Chelmsford. I think I'll stay on in London for a couple of hours."

"Why?" Boyce asked nosily.

"There's an old friend I'd like to call on; someone I haven't seen for years."

Which wasn't strictly true, although only the last part of the remark was a direct lie.

Boyce shrugged.

"Suit yourself," he said in a huffy voice.

They parted at Green Park, where Rudd got off to change to the Jubilee Line, leaving Boyce to go on alone to Holborn, where he'd catch the Central to Liverpool Street.

As the train bore the Sergeant away from the platform towards the tunnel, Rudd caught a passing glimpse of him, his head haloed by the non-smoking sign stuck on the window, his profile still set in an expression of disapproval at this unexpected defection on the part of the Chief Inspector.

CHAPTER THIRTEEN

Harlow Gardens was a turning off Fitzjohn's Avenue, the long road which joined exclusive Hampstead on its hill with the lower, more commercial area round Swiss Cottage.

Rudd got out at the underground station and, having asked directions from a newspaper-seller, turned his back on the traffic roaring up Finchley Road and began the slow climb up the gradient, into the quieter streets which lay behind the main thoroughfare.

At first, Harlow Gardens surprised him. He could not imagine Nina living here. It was lined with large Victorian houses of dark brick; tall, gloomy buildings of such excessive ugliness that he found it hard to understand why she should have chosen, out of the whole of London, to settle in such a place.

Hers, number seven, was no improvement on the others. It was of four storeys, with a semi-basement and five steps leading up to a large porch, so deep and badly lit that Rudd had to bend down and peer at the slotted metal holder containing the residents' name-cards, screwed to the side of the door, in order to read them. Hers was typed, not very accurately. The capital letters on Mrs. N. Gifford and Mr. D. Webb were out of alignment and had been corrected in ink.

He pressed the bell for Flat 3 and waited, wondering if she were at home.

Probably not. It'd been a mistake to come, he decided. He'd've done better to go back to Chelmsford on the train with Boyce.

He had turned away from the front door and was contemplating the houses opposite—like hers, heavy with gables and with low slate lids glowering over porches and bay windows, which gave the facades a frowning intensity—when the intercom grille above the name plate gave a metallic crackle, as if it were clearing its throat. Nina's voice, sounding far away, like someone speaking from outer space across light-years of hissing ether asked, "Is that you, Danny?"

Rudd whipped round.

"No, it's me," he said foolishly, putting his mouth close to the speaker. "Jack Rudd."

There was a small silence and then the tinny, robot voice spoke again.

"I'll let you in. Come up to the first floor."

A buzzer sounded as the lock was released, allowing Rudd to push open the door.

It led into a large, square hall, unfurnished apart from a carved reproduction table on which the residents' mail could be laid out. The touch of fake Tudor was repeated in the oak wainscotting which lined the walls and the massive newel posts and bannisters of the staircase which wouldn't have looked out of place in a baronial hall.

The place smelt old, too, as if the air had been used up years ago and never replaced.

Nina was waiting for him on the upper landing, the door to her flat ajar, clearly pleased as well as surprised to see him. She looked more like the Nina he remembered from the Althorpe days, in an old blouse and skirt, her hair tied back with a bit of ribbon.

She said, "Jack, this is nice!" as if she had always used his Christian name. "Come in. Give me your coat."

In the hall, as he took off his raincoat and she began to hang it up, they both started speaking at the same time.

He began, "I had to come up to London but perhaps I should have . . ." while she was saying, "When the bell rang, I thought it was Danny, forgotten his key again."

". . . phoned you first," Rudd concluded.

"Oh, no," Nina said. "I love surprises."

She smiled at him over her shoulder as she led the way into the drawing-room. As he walked into it, Rudd understood why she had chosen this place in which to live.

The flat occupied the rear part of the upper floor, and had evidently been constructed out of several of the original bedrooms to make a self-contained apartment. The drawing-room, which extended along most of the back of the house, was large and high-ceilinged; it was painted white and equipped with pine bookshelves running along the entire length of one wall. It was more sparsely furnished than the house in Althorpe, as if Nina's taste these days ran to less clutter although Rudd recognised one or two items, such as the oak gate-legged table and a chesterfield covered in worn red leather.

But what caught his immediate attention on entering the room were two other features. One was the long window which looked out over a balcony to a back garden full of trees, which in summer would have filled the room with a moving, leafy light, very much as the rooms in Althorpe House had been.

The other was Max Gifford's portrait of Lilith, which hung on the wall facing this window. It was a nude, full of vibrant life and colour, and yet curiously anonymous. The model lay on a couch with her back to the observer, so that nothing was visible of her except the long taut bow of her spine, the curve of her buttocks, and the shower of dark hair which fell over her shoulders and hid her face.

It had once hung, Rudd remembered, over Max Gifford's bed; a monument to his long-ago passion for Lilith, which had been transferred so tragically to Nina, Lilith's daughter.

Seeing he had noticed it, Nina said quickly, as if she felt some explanation were needed, "I couldn't part with it. It has so much of Max in it."

"Yes, it has," Rudd agreed.

He was wondering if he ought to add something more to this bald statement when Nina went on, covering up any awkwardness and at the same time directing him towards one of the armchairs which had its back to the painting, "Tell me, what are you doing in London?"

"I came up to town to interview Mr. Porlock," he replied, "although that isn't his real name. We got that, and his address, from the man who runs the antique shop in Selhaven. And you were right. The drawing was a Palmer. The pair of them were hoping to negotiate a deal with Miss Kershaw."

"Oh, one of those," Nina said, needing no further explanation. "Someone offers to buy at less than the market value and they split the profit between them. But Miss Kershaw wouldn't have been taken in. She was much too shrewd. Whisky?"

She had gone across to a table on which bottles and glasses were standing, and when Rudd nodded his acceptance, she poured drinks for them both, carrying his glass over to him and taking hers to the chesterfield, where she sat down, her feet tucked under her.

"Was she shrewd?" Rudd asked.

"Yes; about practical things," Nina replied. "Not about people; at least, not about certain people."

"Like Lucy Blake?"

"Oh, her." Nina sounded contemptuous. "Lucy Blake was clever enough to offer Miss Kershaw what she wanted—admiration, not for herself but for her brother."

"And what did Lucy Blake want in return?"

Nina shrugged.

"What do girls like that want? A sense of power? A bit of fun? A buzz—isn't that the word they use?"

"Nothing else? Miss Kershaw gave her a piece of fairly valuable china."

"I don't think that was anything more than a token."

"A token?"

"A physical thing she could take away with her as proof."

"That she'd successfully manipulated Miss Kershaw?"

"Something like that," she agreed.

Rudd sat back in his chair. He supposed he ought not to be

discussing the Kershaw case with Nina Gifford, and yet the occasion seemed right.

Dusk was falling, and the room was full of dwindling light from the after-glow of the sunset, which still lit up the sky behind the trees in the garden. In the shadows, the furniture and pictures had retreated, and the room had taken on an anonymity which he found restful.

Nina, too, was almost invisible, curled up against the arm of the chesterfield, her face nothing more than a pale oval turned towards him.

It occurred to him that she was not unlike Imogen Kershaw—practical, down-to-earth and shrewd; except, as Nina herself had expressed it, where some people were concerned, which was perhaps why she had understood Miss Kershaw so well even after so short an acquaintance. Certainly, out of the people he had so far interviewed, she had given him the clearest picture of the living woman.

As the thought crossed his mind, Nina said, breaking the silence, "Going round the museum the other day, I wondered how she managed. To keep the place going, I mean. There'd be rates. And heating. I can't imagine she made any money at all out of the museum itself. I took a look at the visitors' book. Hardly anyone had been there all year."

She spoke with the certainty of experience, which years of living with Max must have taught her.

Rudd said, "I hadn't thought of that."

It was a point he ought to raise with Osborne. Exactly how had Imogen Kershaw paid her way?

There was a quick rustle as Nina got to her feet to switch on the lamps. In the sudden light, the room and the objects it contained advanced once more into focus, and the tempo of the evening seemed to quicken.

Nina was saying, "By the way, have you eaten?"

"I was going to ask you out to dinner," Rudd replied.

"Oh, I'd love to!" Nina exclaimed. "It's ages since I had a meal out. But I'd better not. Danny said he might be coming

home today. I ought to be here, just in case." As Rudd rose from
his chair as if to leave, she added quickly, "There's no need for
you to go. You can eat here. I've bought plenty of steak and
there's stuff for a salad."

"Thanks. I'd like to very much," Rudd agreed, adding, as
Nina went towards the door, "Anything I can do to help?"

It was the customary offer he always made to his sister when
he was invited to dinner with her and her new husband, and one
which Dorothy invariably refused.

To his surprise, Nina said, "Yes, you can. Bring your glass and
the whisky bottle. We'll have a top up while we get the meal."

The kitchen, unlike the one at Althorpe House, was small and
modern, and yet Nina managed to invest it with some of the
same warmth and bustle he remembered from those earlier days.

"You do the salad," she suggested, sloshing more whisky into
their glasses. "I'll see to the steak. You don't mind garlic, do you?
Max always liked a clove of it mashed into the meat. There's
wine, too. A burgundy; not bad either. The man at the off-
licence recommended it. We can pour a bit of it in to make the
sauce."

As Rudd sliced up tomatoes and shredded endive, Nina put
plates in the oven to warm up, and lit the grille to cook the
frozen chips, a short-cut addition to the meal for which she
didn't apologise.

"Quicker than messing about peeling potatoes," she remarked, getting the steak from the fridge. Looking at it criti-
cally, she went on, in a sudden burst of recklessness, "Let's use it
all up."

"What about Danny?" Rudd asked, gratified at this sign of
generosity for his benefit.

"Oh, sod him. If he comes, I've got a frozen chicken pie he
can have or, if he doesn't fancy that, he can go out for a take-
away. But I don't expect he'll turn up now. He only said he
might. I think he's got some woman in Birmingham and looking
for a job was only an excuse to go up there to see her."

Rudd prudently made no comment on this, but asked instead, "Do you want me to deal with the wine?"

"Would you?" Nina said. "You'll find the corkscrew in the top drawer over here. I suppose I should have opened it earlier to let it breathe. Chambréd, isn't that the word? Max always said I didn't know a thing about wine."

"I don't suppose it really matters," Rudd assured her.

To get to the drawer, he had to pass behind her as she stood at the gas stove. She had pushed up the sleeves of her blouse, revealing the upper part of her arms, the flesh firm and round, and faintly stippled with little brown flecks like the shell of an egg. He caught a breath of her scent; the heavy, more medicinal odour of the whisky was overlaid by a sweeter fragrance which seemed to come from her hair. He felt unexpectedly roused by her proximity, the intimacy of the small kitchen and the shared domestic chores.

Was she aware of it, too? She might have been because later— at the end of the meal, which they had eaten at the gate-legged table in the drawing-room—she suddenly asked in a gap in the conversation which up to that moment had been about general matters, "You never married, did you?"

The question took him aback, and his first reaction was to brush it aside with some non-committal, half-joking remark about not ever having found the time.

She seemed to be expecting this response. She had lifted her glass as if, should he evade the question, she would drink a little of the wine before steering the conversation back to a less personal topic.

Instead, he heard himself saying, "I hoped to once but it didn't work out."

She said, "I'm sorry. Perhaps I shouldn't have asked."

"I don't mind," he replied, and then quickly correcting himself, "At least, I don't mind as much as I did a couple of months ago." As he said it, he was surprised to find that this was true. "Her name's Marion. She's a pathologist who I worked with once on a case. I don't suppose there's anything unique about the situation. I wanted to marry; she didn't want to commit herself to any long-term relationship. In the end, she moved to another job, miles away. We kept in touch at first but I haven't heard from her for months now. It's possibly better that way. I don't know."

"I'm sorry," Nina said again.

She seemed genuinely distressed at having raised the subject. Across the table, Rudd could see her bottom lip had softened, and for some reason, the sight of it made him feel harder and more sure of his own reactions.

"You coped with Max's death," he told her, more harshly than he had intended. "I suppose I'll do the same."

"It's not easy," Nina said. "And I can't promise that you'll ever get over it; not completely, that is. There are days even now when I hear or see something—it could be anything, someone talking on a bus, or that very special light of early morning—and I think, 'Oh, God, I wish Max was here! He'd've enjoyed that.' "

"And the other days?" Rudd asked.

"Oh, the other days!" Nina smiled and raised a shoulder. "You get through them somehow." She had finished her wine and, putting down her glass, began to collect up the used plates and dishes with a briskness that put an end to the conversation. "I'll make coffee."

"And I'll wash up," Rudd offered.

"No, you won't," Nina retorted. "I don't mind a man giving a hand with the cooking but I hate anyone helping with the washing-up. I'll do it later."

Over coffee, she fetched from the bookshelves a volume of Samuel Palmer reproductions—which had once belonged to Max Gifford—for him to look at. Her intention was, Rudd assumed, to keep the rest of the evening on a less personal level.

Turning the pages, he could understand Nina's certainty, on first seeing it that the drawing in the Kershaw museum had been a Palmer. The style had a character of its own; not unlike Max's, he realised, although superficially their work was entirely different. And yet both of them possessed that ability to convey the essence of a landscape, or, in Gifford's case, a person, with a few strokes of a brush or pen, which not only captured the soul of the subject but also something of the artist's as well.

He glanced up at the wall opposite on which was hanging one of the few other pictures by Gifford which Nina had chosen to display. It, too, was a drawing, and one which, unlike the portrait of Lilith, made little claim on the attention. Perhaps that was why Nina had selected it.

It was a sketch made in crayon, depicting a woman, stripped to the waist, washing herself at a basin set on a table. He guessed it was of Nina, made years ago when she was much younger, although there was little attempt to delineate the features in any detail. In making it, Gifford's purpose seemed to have been merely to rough out a quick working sketch. And yet there was such a loving tenderness in the swelling curve of the breasts, and in the manner in which he had caught the young woman's total absorption in her task, that Rudd felt uncomfortably like a voyeur, intruding on an intensely private moment.

He left shortly afterwards, making as his excuse that he wanted to catch a particular train from Liverpool Street station, although he had no idea of the timetable.

Nina accompanied him into the hall, edging past him as he put on his coat to open the front door.

She was saying, "I've enjoyed this evening, Jack. I'm so glad you came."

It was the first time she had used his Christian name since his arrival, and he realised that throughout the whole evening, both of them had scrupulously avoided addressing each other directly.

He heard himself replying, "So have I, Nina."

And then, without quite knowing he was about to do anything of the sort, he leaned forward and kissed her cheek.

It came as much of a surprise to him as to her. For a few moments, they stood together in the narrow hall by the coat pegs, their faces touching. He felt her skin against his lips and the weight of one of her breasts pressing on his arm, as he breathed in her scent again.

She gave a little gasp—but whether of consternation or pleasure, he could not tell.

Without looking at her, he went out onto the landing where, a space having been established between them, he turned to face her.

She was standing in the open doorway, still holding on to the catch. The light, which was behind her, made it difficult for him to read her expression.

"May I ring you?" he asked.

"Yes, of course," she said. "You've got my number, haven't you?"

And that was that.

He raised his hand and began to descend the stairs, remembering only when he was three steps down to call out, "And thanks for the meal."

She was in the act of closing the door but she nodded and smiled through the gap, acknowledging the remark.

Outside it was raining, a fine, persistent drizzle which had varnished the pavements black, the light from the street lamps brushed across them like gold lacquer.

Walking quickly through the rain towards the underground station, Rudd thought over the evening with Nina, concentrating on the earlier part. He was aware that he was deliberately postponing any consideration of that moment of parting.

The room. The meal. The book of Palmer reproductions. Nina curled up at one end of the big chesterfield. These images were more real than the journey, although part of his conscious mind remained alert enough for him to buy a ticket and take in the names of the stations along the route to Baker Street, where he changed onto the Circle line.

Emerging out of the underground at Liverpool Street, he walked up the long ramp which led on to the main-line terminus. Here he paused under the great arch of the roof to look up at the departure board.

He had missed the fast train to Norwich—first stop Shenfield and then Chelmsford—by ten minutes. The next, for Harwich, left in a quarter of an hour. He could catch that.

Standing there, studying the board, he saw the letters and figures in the adjoining section begin to revolve as a train for the other line to Northminster was announced. It was the 9:25, calling at Wythorpe and Selhaven; the same train, he realised, that Osborne must have caught on the night of Imogen Kershaw's murder.

So Osborne had stood here, as Rudd was doing, having, like him, missed one train and been forced to wait for the next.

Rudd glanced about him. There wasn't much to do to while away the time. The bookshop and the kiosks were closed and the concourse was largely occupied by people merely standing or sitting about in that state of limbo which any terminal building seems to generate. A man lay asleep on a bench. A couple was holding hands under the clock, the grief of imminent parting eloquent in their stance.

It was only an illusion, but the rain seemed to have penetrated inside the structure, fogging up the lights and smearing the floor with moisture. A damp wind, blowing in through one of the entrances, added to the impression of a place open to the elements.

Plunging his hands into his raincoat pockets, Rudd walked up and down, averting his eyes from the couple who were kissing with a hurried, almost frenzied, intensity, until the girl broke away and began running towards one of the platform barriers. Carriage doors slammed. A train began to pull out, slinking away backwards under the girders of the roof, its lighted windows compressed by the perspective into one moving, illuminated block.

As he watched it leave, Rudd was suddenly and absurdly reminded of the feel of Nina's face against his, and the scent of her hair.

His own train arrived soon afterwards. Getting into a carriage, he found a copy of the *Evening News* which a previous occupant had left behind on the seat and which he read throughout the journey from cover to cover, including the film reviews and the football results on the back page.

Beyond the windows, the outskirts of London slipped past—first, the anonymous rear facades of terrace houses; then the new Council estates, deserted in the rain. A canal glittered briefly. After that, there was the darkness of the countryside, broken occasionally by a lighted window or the lamps of stations where the train didn't stop, and where no-one was waiting.

At Chelmsford, Rudd carefully refolded the newspaper and left it on the seat before following the other departing passengers down the steps to the booking-hall, where he turned right for the taxi-rank.

The house was, of course, in darkness when he let himself in. Switching on lights and tramping through to the kitchen to put the kettle on for tea, he was conscious that the sounds he made had disturbed some secret life in which the rooms had been participating during his absence. It was as if, on returning, he had to make an effort to re-establish his presence and claim these empty spaces, however familiar, in the same way as, when putting on an old coat, one might flex the shoulders to remould the fabric to one's frame.

Once that was done, he felt at ease, carrying the tray of tea-things through to the sitting-room, where he sat down in his usual chair, prepared to spend what was left of the evening in pleasant idleness.

There was no post; no messages on the answer-phone; nothing to stop him from simply sitting there and letting his mind go blank, a rare indulgence.

Instead, he found his thoughts turning once again to the day's events; not so much to Nina, although she was at the back of his mind as a warm presence which he no longer felt the need to summon up.

He thought instead of Chadwick and of the glittering look about him when he had spoken of the Palmer drawing; he thought of Scott, too, turning away from the shelf of files in the manuscript room, denying he had noticed anything wrong about them. And then, oddly enough, he remembered the image he had conjured up on Liverpool Street station of Osborne waiting for the train to Selhaven.

It kept intruding on his thoughts, and he had no idea why it kept recurring with such exasperating regularity.

He was trying to pin down the reason when the phone rang.

It was Archer, speaking as usual too close to the mouthpiece in that low, conspiratorial tone which always made the Chief Inspector feel that he was being crowded into a corner.

"Listen," Archer said. "About that mate of yours you mentioned the other evening. Know who I mean? We think he might be making a little trip tonight. Do you want to be in on it?"

"What do you think?" Rudd demanded without any hesitation.

At once, he was alert, his mind clear; whatever vague image it had held concerning Osborne entirely banished.

"High tide's at 1:30. If you could get yourself to the landing-point by that time, a colleague of mine, name of Neal, will pick you up. He'll fill you in with the details. Take the main road out of Selhaven. About a mile past the T-junction, you'll see a turning off to your left. It's sign-posted 'Potter's Farm.' At the far end of the lane, there's a small jetty where you can leave the car. Neal'll meet you there. And try not to advertise yourself if you can help it, Jack. We don't want the farmer phoning the fuzz about a strange car seen in the area, do we?"

"Right," Rudd said. "I get you."

"And wear something warm," Archer added. "It could be a long, cold night."

He rang off, leaving Rudd smiling broadly as, replacing his own receiver, he pounded up the stairs to change out of his good suit and rummage through the wardrobe for an old duffel coat which he hadn't worn for years, glad that he'd persuaded his sister not to throw it away.

In the excitement of the chase to come, he forgot about Scott, Chadwick, Osborne, even Nina.

Things were moving at last.

And about bloody time, too.

CHAPTER FOURTEEN

Even though he was looking out for it, Rudd nearly missed the turning. It was tucked away on his left, between hedges which seemed to continue without a gap. It was only the white-painted finger-post, suddenly illuminated in the headlights, which gave him warning to brake, change down and ease the car into the opening.

The lane ran downhill for about half a mile. Its surface of packed stones and flints made the driving relatively easy, and he was able to let the car roll forward in second with the engine revving gently. Although the moon was obscured by clouds, there was enough diffused glimmer of brightness for him to see with only the side-lights on. Once his eyes grew accustomed to the darkness, he realised that the sky was, in fact, lighter than the land, stretching out in front of him in a shifting cloudscape which almost filled the windscreen. Below it, the fields seemed very black and static, a narrow rim of horizon, ruler-straight, broken only by the occasional bulging contour of a tree.

At the bottom of the hill, the hard-surfaced lane swerved abruptly off to the right towards Potter's farm. He could see the house and its outbuildings a little distance away, a more complex silhouette composed of rectangular blocks and triangles, all in total darkness; not a light to be seen.

The lane continued ahead of him, a mere farm-track now of deeply-rutted earth, forcing him to drop down into bottom gear and to keep gunning the engine to prevent it from stalling.

He smelt the river before he saw it. He was driving with the window down, watching his near side where an occasional streak of pale light, reflected back from the sky, suggested a water-filled drainage ditch. If he got his wheels stuck in that, he'd never get the bloody car out, he thought.

The river odour came gusting in through the window, complex but unmistakable: mud, rotting vegetation with a cleaner, saltier back-taste of the sea. And then he saw it only yards in front of him—the black water running fast, chopped into brighter darkness by the wind.

A torch flashed, illuminating briefly the shining rail of a boat, which remained stamped on his retina as a brilliant after-image for several seconds, dazzling his vision. He drew up, turned off the lights and engine and got out, straining forward to see through the bar of light across his eyes.

The torch shone again, pointing downwards onto planking, and he edged cautiously forward to a rickety landing-stage which sounded hollow under his feet. Water slapped rhythmically against wooden piles and the side of a boat.

The next moment, a hand was stretched out into the circle of torch-light and, grabbing it, he stepped forward and down into the police launch.

A voice out of a bulky shape in front of him said "Welcome aboard, sir" perfectly seriously, as if Rudd were an admiral being escorted onto the deck of a destroyer. "We'll be casting off any minute now. It'll take us about half an hour to get into position. Our target's about ten minutes ahead of us down river. Want to come inside?"

An arm was flourished, indicating a dimly lit cabin containing other figures. It looked crowded and claustrophobic and too unfamiliar.

"Sergeant Neal, isn't it? Thanks all the same but I'll stay on deck," Rudd replied, hoping to God he'd used the correct expression.

But whether outside, on deck, or whatever, at least there was air and space.

While they had been speaking, the launch had sidled away from the landing-stage into mid-stream, engines quietly throbbing.

There was, thank the Lord, surprisingly little sense of movement, only a steady vibration underfoot and the low band of landscape moving gently backwards, slipping away into the darkness behind, while the sky moved still more slowly, its huge arc wheeling above him by leisurely degrees.

It was curiously silent, too, despite the regular pulse of the engines. Behind it, Rudd could hear the water running and the wind hissing in the reeds which lined the banks. The low voices of the men, coming from the cabin, and the occasional disembodied chatter from the radio seemed an intrusion into the great silence and emptiness.

Shortly afterwards Neal came ducking out of the cabin to join him.

"I don't know how much Detective Inspector Archer told you, sir . . ."

"Not much," Rudd replied. "He didn't want to go into detail over the phone."

"Then I'll try and put you in the picture. It's a liaison job between us, Customs at Harwich, and the Dutch authorities. They've been suspicious of a fishing boat for several months now but haven't been able to get anything definite on it. After your tip-off about Kemp, Detective Inspector Archer got in touch with them. It seemed there was a possible connection so we put a couple of surveillance men on to Kemp. They reported he'd taken fuel on board his boat late this afternoon. As the Dutch boat was also getting ready to leave harbour, it looked as if there might be a contact arranged, one worth following up by anybody's book. And it'd have to be at high tide for Kemp to leave his mooring. As his boat's too small to risk going far out to sea, we're counting on the stuff being passed over somewhere in the estuary—God knows where; it could be any point along the coast. There's a Customs launch standing off in the hope of making an interception, as well as one of our own high-speed dories. The Dutch are shadowing their suspect but keeping well back until after the hand-over's made. We're acting as back-up in case Kemp gets suspicious and tries to make a run for it back to

Selhaven or they miss him and he slips away down river with the stuff on board. Either way, we pick him up. We're making for Windle Creek, off Fowlers' Marsh, close to the estuary. We'll lie up there and wait for developments."

"What do you think the stuff is?" Rudd asked. "Heroin? Cocaine?"

Neal shrugged.

"Could be either, although it's most probably cocaine now the crack merchants have moved in. And at twenty-three thousand quid a kilo, it needn't be a large drop to make the trip worthwhile. Kemp's too small an operator anyway for it to be a really massive haul."

"What's Kemp likely to make on it?"

"Two to three thousand a kilo; that's the usual rate. Not bad, is it, for a night's work?"

He disappeared once more inside the cabin as the radio broke in, returning after about ten minutes to announce, "We're almost there, sir. Windle Creek's coming up to starboard. You may even see some of the action if you use these." He handed Rudd a pair of night binoculars, adding, as the Chief Inspector hung them round his neck, "And they've got an interception point on the radar, thank God, otherwise it can be like playing hunt the slipper in the dark. It's just off Deacon's Sand, not far out in the estuary. The Dutch boat made the drop about quarter of an hour ago attached to a marker. They've let him start the run back to Holland where the Dutch customs will pick him up."

The tempo of the engines had altered, thrusting more powerfully into reverse as the launch began to edge backwards. Water churned white and the landscape shifted. Rudd, tensing his legs against this change in direction, saw the banks had swung about before closing in along the sides of a narrower stretch of water, edged with reeds. The wind had changed direction, too. It was blowing now against the side of his face, bringing with it the smell of the open sea.

Raising the glasses, he tried to focus them against the motion of the boat, clamping his elbows against his sides and feeling for the first time a faint nausea as the view swooped suddenly towards him, startling him by its proximity and its swaying movement. The horizon, a dark line, tilted and rocked disconcertingly. Below it lay what he imagined must be the sea, glittering with its own heave and swell, the white caps of the waves racing towards him.

At nearer view, the reeds confused the image. A blurred forest of blades criss-crossed his vision, but by raising the glasses cautiously millimetre by millimetre, he was able to see beyond them to a flatter, broader expanse which seemed motionless. Not the sea, then. Mud-banks perhaps. Or sand. It was impossible to tell.

Neal, his own binoculars to his eyes, was stabbing a finger—left! left! There was an urgency in the gesture which, as Rudd turned in that direction, was echoed by the staccato voice rattling over the radio inside the cabin with the same excited velocity.

And then he saw it, in a sequence of rapid images which succeeded one another like stills taken by flashlight and exposed momentarily on a dark screen and which out-paced his own mental processes as he struggled to interpret them.

A round, orange-coloured shape bobbed—a head? A swimmer drowning? It was lost as the bulk of a boat cut across his view. He had time to recognise the blue flashing of Kemp's cabin cruiser, the "Lucy Fair," before a low hull, prow raised, came racing past its stern and the picture was broken up in a flurry of spray so close, it seemed, that he stepped back involuntarily and lost the image as it veered off out of sight. When he picked it up again, the scene was brilliantly lit by the powerful beam of a searchlight. The area on which the glasses were concentrating was crowded with craft, their prows jostling together and relatively static so that he was able to let the binoculars pass over them, picking out details—the lean outline of the customs launch, the searchlight mounted on its cabin roof, a figure in the act of leaping across the gap to the deck of the "Lucy Fair," the police dory turning slowly, someone leaning over the side and grappling in the water close to the orange head—which he saw, with a sense of relief, was nothing more than a marker buoy.

Voices drifted back to him, ridiculously far away considering the nearness of the image and he realised that he had been aware before of distant shouts from a loud hailer, which he had heard but had not properly registered.

The radio was clattering again inside the cabin, and Neal ducked down to answer it, saying jubilantly as he went, "We've got a take! Bloody marvellous!"

He was back within minutes to announce, "They're taking Kemp's boat back into Selhaven with the stuff on board. We're acting as escort."

They saw it passing the entrance to the creek about a quarter of an hour later, the silhouette of its wheel-house moving slowly past the skyline. Lights were on inside the cabin, but at that distance it was impossible to distinguish individuals, only heads massed against the glass. Two more figures were standing on deck, cut off at the waist by the far bank, their upper torsos carried smoothly along with the forward motion of the boat.

The engines of the launch had been started, and as the "Lucy Fair" passed in mid-stream, their own craft eased out to follow, bouncing a little in its wake, and picking up in the night wind the fumes of its diesel.

Neal was talking, describing the encounter, still animated by the success.

Rudd listened intermittently, face turned out of the wind and concentrating rather on the landscape ahead of him, where the lights of Selhaven should be coming into view any bloody minute.

Now that it was all over, he was aching with cold, and stiff with the effort of bracing himself against the unaccustomed tip and sway of the deck.

". . . tucked in round the point . . . ," Neal was saying. ". . . the dory came up on their blind side . . . bloody cracking bit of timing . . ."

"Yes, cracking," Rudd said, trying to match Neal's enthusiasm and then, with genuine excitement, "Isn't that Selhaven over to our left?" remembering too late that he should have said "port." Or was it "starboard"? He was past caring.

There was Selhaven, the low hill on which it was built lifting up against the sky and scattered with tiny points of light.

Neal had disappeared again inside the cabin, although Rudd barely noticed his departure. He was watching those distant lights draw closer, with all the fervour of a lone yachtsman finally making it to harbour after a single-handed crossing of the Atlantic.

They advanced with incredible slowness, inch by inch, it seemed, at first merely bunching randomly together, and then as the launch rounded the bend in the river, sorting themselves out into patterns, the straighter lines of the street lamps interspersed with darker spaces where only the occasional lighted window broke the blackness. The slopes of roofs and the tower of the church became visible against the sky. Finally, it was possible to make out the harbour itself, with a few sparse lamps strung out along its front, the elongated reflections wobbling uneasily in the ink-black water, the prows of the boats at anchor jogging up and down among them.

The launch swung about and reversed into a mooring. A rope was thrown to someone ashore, and Rudd was hauled up onto the concrete footway, where he stood stamping his feet to get the blood moving again—and to assure himself that the ground was indeed solid.

A uniformed PC, huddled up in a greatcoat, emerged from the shadows.

There was a car waiting to take him to the police station. Was the Chief Inspector ready to leave?

Was he ready? The prospect of a warm interior and almost certainly tea—and if there wasn't, he'd pull rank and demand it—was comfort indeed.

The car was parked at the side of the Barge. As they walked towards it, Rudd saw the "Lucy Fair" moored a little distance away and Archer, already on shore, standing with his hands on his hips in an attitude of impatience, waiting for the others to disembark before the Chief Inspector climbed into the back seat and the car drove away.

At the police station, it might have been early evening. All the lights were on, people were moving about, telephones were ringing.

Coming through the swing doors into the reception area, Rudd drew in great lungfuls of warm air. And there was tea. But not quite yet. Bayliss, meeting him at the entrance, was saying, "There's hot drinks laid on. . . . ," when the doors opened and Archer came in, his face jubilant, followed by five men in oilskins, one of them hugging to his chest like a rugby ball a black plastic-wrapped parcel, the group of Drug Squad officers forming a small scrum about two other figures.

They were hustled so quickly past him down the corridor towards the interview rooms that Rudd caught only a glimpse of them, the fluorescent lights gleaming on Lucy Blake's fair hair and on Kemp's profile. And on the collar of his waterproof jacket, turned up and glistening as if it were wet through. It seemed to draw the Chief Inspector's attention, for he kept his gaze fixed on it until Kemp disappeared from sight.

Archer, grinning like a schoolboy, had broken away from the others and come over to where Rudd and Bayliss were standing.

"See any of the action?" he demanded, but, not giving Rudd time to reply, rattled on, "Went like bloody clockwork. Ten kilos of the stuff! Worth about a quarter of a million. And almost certainly cocaine. We haven't managed to screw much out of the pair of them yet. Kemp says he doesn't know any names or addresses. He just hands the stuff over at the Ring of Bells. Pushes it under the partition in the gents'—I ask you!—and the payment for the trip gets passed to him the same way. It's so simple it's frigging cheeky."

The next moment he had gone, sprinting off down the corridor like a man with a bus to catch.

Bayliss was saying, "If you want to pick up your car later wherever it was you left it, I can lay on transport," and was surprised when the Chief Inspector, who hadn't evidently been listening, asked unexpectedly, "What was the name of the PC who sent in that report on Scott?"

"You mean Fowles?"

"Yes, that's him. Is he on the beat tonight? Any chance of you contacting him for me?"

"Of course," Bayliss said, as if the request were perfectly consequential.

As they walked up the stairs to Bayliss's office, Rudd continued, feeling he owed the man some explanation, "It's important I talk to him as soon as possible. Ask him to suggest somewhere we can meet that's convenient in the town centre."

But only part of his mind was concentrated on these practical considerations. Underneath this rational layer, his thoughts were racing forward.

It had to be the answer because no other explanation made sense. Like a magnet acting on iron filings, it drew together all the scattered scraps of information and half-formed ideas towards a central conclusion. He could feel the force of the logic which seemed to function without any conscious effort on his part.

First there was Nina's remark about how Imogen Kershaw managed. Then his own memory of the great arched roof of Liverpool Street station together with something Chadwick had said. And finally, Scott turning away from that shelf in the manuscript room—the last piece to slide into place.

As Bayliss contacted Fowles on his personal radio, a PC brought in tea, which Rudd gulped down quickly, feeling the hot liquid scald its way into his stomach. There was no time to enjoy it. He hadn't even bothered to unbutton his duffel coat.

It was hardly worth it anyway. As soon as Bayliss had announced, "Fowles says he'll meet you in five minutes in the doorway of the post office in the High Street," Rudd had put down his cup and was off, taking the steps two at a time.

Fowles was already there when he arrived, peering out of the post office entrance and moving from foot to foot as he waited.

Apart from him, the High Street was deserted—the grilles down over the windows of the jeweller's, the Wimpy bar closed and the King's Head showing a few dimmed lights in its foyer. Only the orange standards on the pedestrian crossing pulsing on and off, and the litter bowling along the gutter from the take-away, gave the street any animation.

Fowles seemed inclined to turn the impromptu meeting into a formal conference. As his hand came up in a salute, Rudd crowded him back into the doorway out of the wind.

"Listen," he said. "You were on duty on Wednesday, the night Miss Kershaw was murdered."

"That's right, sir. I put in a report about seeing Mr. Scott coming out of the front gate of the museum . . ."

"I read it," Rudd broke in impatiently. "That's not what I'm on about right now. What time did it start to rain that night?"

"Rain?" asked Fowles as if he'd never heard of the stuff. He seemed bewildered that a Detective Chief Inspector, dressed like a down-and-out in a disgraceful duffel coat, should insist on holding this interview in a doorway at that God-awful hour in the morning to talk about what the weather had been like three nights before.

He said carefully, "Well, I'm not exactly sure, sir; not to the precise moment. It was while I was checking on the lock-up garages behind the maisonettes in Burford Road. There's been complaints about vandals . . ."

"What time?" Rudd demanded, resisting an urge to take Fowles by the collar and shake the information out of him.

Fowles seemed aware of the Chief Inspector's anger, for he took a quick breath and came to the point.

"It'd be about twenty past ten, sir."

"You're certain?"

"Not to the exact minute, like I said. But it's near enough. About ten minutes later, I heard the clock on All Hallows strike the half hour. The rain had eased off a bit by then. It was a heavy old downpour while it lasted although it was all over in less than fifteen minutes."

"And you saw Mr. Scott at quarter past eleven that same evening?"

"That's right, sir. I did check my watch that time; not that I suspected Mr. Scott of any funny business. It just seemed a bit odd, him coming from the museum when the place was in darkness."

"Yes," said Rudd, appearing to agree. Then abruptly, he asked, "Where's the station?"

Fowles seemed to have grown accustomed to the Chief Inspector's unconventional manner, for without any hesitation, he lifted a uniformed arm.

"Straight down to the bottom of the High Street, sir, and turn right. You'll see the sign for it."

"Thanks," Rudd said, and went loping off in that direction.

The station, like the High Street, was deserted, the ticket office closed, although all the lights were on in the booking-hall. A train had evidently not long departed, for as Rudd walked past the barrier and on to the platform in search of someone, he found a solitary porter piling up a trolley with bundles of newspapers which had presumably been off-loaded from a London train.

"Mind if I look round?" Rudd asked, producing his ID card.

"Help yourself, mate," replied the porter, too experienced to show any surprise.

All the same, he broke off from his task to watch, as the Chief Inspector tramped down to the far end of the platform.

Whatever it was he wanted to examine, it didn't take long.

He stood for a couple of minutes, hands in pockets, at the point where the platform sloped down to the rails, turning his head round to look first at the ticket barrier, and then at the low embankment and fence which separated the near platform from the adjoining car-park.

Then he strolled back again.

He had a couple of questions to ask, neither of which took long to answer, the last being directions for the quickest way to a certain road in the town.

After that, he left.

There was a light on in the hall when Rudd arrived at the house, so the chances were someone was up, he thought, as he rang the bell, although he doubted if he were expected.

Shortly afterwards, the door opened and Ambrose Scott appeared on the threshold, his expression, to the Chief Inspector's surprise, one of profound relief.

CHAPTER FIFTEEN

Scott said, "Oh, thank God it's you, Chief Inspector. I was going to phone you. Come in. Come in."

He flapped an arm, inviting the Chief Inspector into the hall.

"Where's Mr. Osborne?" Rudd demanded, following Scott, who had gone ahead of him, into the drawing-room where the lamps were turned on and the curtains drawn. A tray of used tea-things and a couple of dirty glasses, together with a whisky decanter, standing on a low table in front of a log fire which had been reduced to glowing charcoal, suggested that the room had been occupied for some time by two people—Osborne and Scott, Rudd suspected, although there was no sign of Osborne.

Scott seemed in no hurry to answer the Chief Inspector's question. Folding himself down into an armchair by the side of the fireplace, he leaned forward to place a couple of logs on top of the mound of embers, lifting them with the poker to allow the air to circulate, and watching as the small flames kindled under them.

"Where's Mr. Osborne?" Rudd repeated more loudly.

Scott twisted round to look up at him. But instead of answering the question, he said, his voice quite flat as if he were stating the obvious, "You've come to arrest Clive for Imogen's murder. What put you on to him? I only realised the truth myself when I saw those files in the manuscript room. Imogen wouldn't have left them like that. And no ordinary burglar would have bothered to move them. It had to be someone connected with William's past. Even then I didn't want to believe it was Clive. I sat for hours trying to persuade myself I was wrong. After all, he had an alibi. He'd been in London until late Wednesday evening and had gone straight home from the train so he seemed to be in the clear. And then this evening, I came round here to talk to him and he told me everything."

Rudd sat down on the chair opposite Scott so that their faces were on a level. The man was in shock, he realised. It affected people in different ways. Some wept or became violent. Others, like Scott, retreated into a state bordering on catalepsy, in which they spoke and acted with apparent normality. It was only the face and the voice, both fixed and expressionless, which revealed the depth of the trauma from which they were suffering. Scott was like an automaton which had been wound up, and which would go on functioning until the point of collapse.

More gently, Rudd said, "Look, Mr. Scott, I need to know where Mr. Osborne is. Can you tell me?"

Scott gazed about him with a vaguely puzzled air, as if expecting to find Osborne seated somewhere in the room. Then, recovering a little, he replied, "He's gone. He went out ages ago. We were talking, I remember, for hours. Then he said, 'There's something I've got to see to, Ambrose. I shan't be long.' I stayed here. He didn't want Mrs. Wharton to be left alone in the house. Clive persuaded her to take a sleeping-tablet before she went to bed so that she wouldn't be kept awake by us talking down here."

"Did he take the car?" Rudd asked.

"Yes, I think so. I heard it driving away."

"And do you know where he's gone?"

Scott looked directly across at the Chief Inspector, and for a moment the blank look in his eyes was replaced by a much more aware expression, which vanished as instantly.

"I've no idea," he said. "He could be anywhere."

He was probably speaking the truth, Rudd thought, although, seeing Scott's face, he began to be seriously concerned about Osborne's safety. He wondered if it also explained Scott's relief when he had come to the door and had seen it was only the Chief Inspector standing in the porch. Had he feared that it was

Osborne who had returned, whom he'd have to turn over to the police for the murder of Imogen Kershaw?

"I'm going to make a couple of phone calls," Rudd told him, getting up from the chair. "Wait here. I shan't be long."

He used the telephone in the hall, keeping his voice low so that neither Scott nor Mrs. Wharton—asleep upstairs under the influence of the sleeping-tablet, he assumed—could overhear him. The first was to Bayliss at the Selhaven police station, explaining the situation to him briefly, and requesting that all mobile units should be alerted to watch out for Osborne's grey BMW. He also asked for a doctor and a WPC to be sent to Osborne's house. The second call got Boyce out of bed.

As soon as the Sergeant had assured him that he was on his way, Rudd replaced the receiver and returned to the drawing-room, where he found Scott still seated in exactly the same position in which he had left him, his long frame huddled forward over the fire and his eyes fixed on the flames which were beginning to feel their way round the base of the logs. It was as if he were drawing warmth and strength from their meagre blaze, even though the house, with the central heating full on, was uncomfortably hot. Rudd had abandoned his duffel coat in the hall.

He resumed his seat again opposite Scott, prepared to sit it out in silence if that was what the man preferred. Scott was in no condition to be forced into making a statement but, as Rudd settled back in the chair, Scott, without moving his eyes from the fire, began to speak in the same low, mechanical voice with which he had first greeted the Chief Inspector.

"You must understand," he said, "that Clive didn't go to the house intending to kill Imogen. He only wanted to talk to her. He'd called round to see her earlier that morning on the way to the station and she'd told him about her plan to republish William's books. She wanted to discuss the financial side of it with him and how much it would cost to pay for private printing if no publisher was willing to re-issue them. Clive would have been the best person for her to ask, of course. He was a businessman and he'd helped to handle her finances since William's death. There wasn't much opportunity to discuss the idea in detail at that first visit; Clive had his train to catch. But he told me that all the time he was in London, he kept thinking about Imogen's scheme. It wasn't really practical. Even I realised that. No publisher was going to want to take the books and Imogen couldn't have afforded to pay for even one of them to be printed privately. But she'd never thought straight about William. I don't think any of us had. He created his own obsession, centred on himself, and all of us were sucked into it, Clive included, although at least Clive managed to break free—at a price."

He paused to look across again at the Chief Inspector, his expression more open, almost daring—as if, having exhausted his energy, he needed help to revitalise that inward mechanism which kept him going.

"What price?" Rudd asked.

"His marriage," Scott replied. "William and Clive were once lovers. Did you know that?"

"Go on," Rudd said, giving a little nod to indicate that he had suspected it. Nina had given him the first clue by referring to Osborne as a 'golden lad,' even though she had not been aware at the time of the significance of her remark. Osborne himself had supplied the other. During Rudd's interview with him, he had recalled his relationship with William Kershaw with a warmth of genuine feeling which Scott had not shown when speaking of his own friendship with the man.

The small gesture of the head was enough to re-animate Scott, who turned away once more to the fire, his bony hands clutching at his knees, as he resumed his account.

"Nothing was ever said, of course. But all of us knew, even Imogen although I don't think she faced up to the truth until after William's death. It was different in those days. No-one dreamed of mentioning such things. What's that quotation? Something about 'the love that dares not speak its name'? And Imogen didn't want to acknowledge it for quite a different reason of her own. She was in love with Clive herself. Dear Christ, what a mess!"

"And that's why Clive married?" Rudd suggested. "To escape?"

"It was a disaster from the start," Scott continued. "Sexually. Emotionally. Psychologically. It killed something in Clive. I saw the light go out of him. But deep down, he'd always been a conventional person. He wanted to be accepted socially, to be successful, and that's what marriage to Laura gave him—a place in society, respectability, security—none of which William could offer him. It ended his relationship with William, of course. That was the intention. And to give William his due, he accepted Clive's marriage fairly philosophically. There was a meeting between them just before Clive announced his engagement to Laura. I don't know exactly what was said. Clive broke down when he tried to tell me about it this evening but I gathered William returned all the love letters which Clive had sent him and which Clive later burnt. They never met again although William appointed Clive as one of the executors to his will and Clive went to his funeral so I suppose you could say there was a sort of reconciliation. Clive's wife died a couple of years later. It was after her death that Clive began to pick up the threads again with Imogen—out of guilt, I imagine. He said that he felt he owed her as well as William something after all those years of friendship—a mistake, of course. He should have steered clear of her."

"Why?" Rudd asked, although he had already guessed the answer.

"Because there was a price to pay—literally. I don't think Imogen had ever quite forgiven Clive for his defection as she saw it. He'd betrayed William. He'd also betrayed her. And so he had to be punished. That may be too strong a word to use although there'd always been a hard quality about her—determined, unflinching. Once she'd made up her mind, nothing would persuade her to change it. After William's death, she set up the museum as a memorial to him and that was where Clive came in. I think he entered the situation quite willingly, knowing what it meant but seeing it as a kind of expiation."

"He helped her finance it," Rudd said.

Ambrose Scott gave that abrupt, cawing laugh of his.

"What else could he offer except money? That's all he had. And Imogen accepted it as if it were her due. She couldn't have afforded to run the place on her own. She had very little money apart from her pension, and there were all kinds of expenses involved in keeping the house going. William left hardly anything. Even when he was alive, his books hadn't been all that successful financially and they've been out of print for years. So someone had to help her out with the bills; Clive, of course. I was naive. I should have realised it."

And so should I, Rudd thought. It had taken Nina to see it. He hadn't made the connection at the time, although he should have suspected something of the sort during his interview with Osborne when the state of Imogen Kershaw's financial affairs had been discussed. He could understand now Osborne's reluctance to discuss them.

Out loud, he said, "What happened on Wednesday evening when Clive went back to the museum? There was a quarrel, wasn't there? Was it about money?"

"That was the apparent reason although for both of them it was merely a catalyst, something tangible they could both use to express all the other old bitternesses and resentments which had been building up over the years and which neither of them really wanted to bring out into the open. Clive, as I said, had spent the day in London, thinking over the scheme to reprint William's books. He knew he'd be asked to finance it but he was reconciled to that. It seemed a relatively small price to pay. When he called round at the house later that evening . . ." Scott broke off suddenly to ask, "You realise he caught the earlier train?"

"Yes, I know that," Rudd told him. It was not the moment to explain exactly how he'd come to that conclusion and, anxious not to distract Scott from his statement, he gave another small nod, encouraging the man to continue.

To his relief, Scott resumed his account.

"Imogen had been working in the manuscript room. When Clive rang the bell, she came downstairs and let him in at the front door. They went into the sitting-room where, Clive said, they talked fairly amicably to begin with. She explained her scheme in more detail—how she intended approaching a few publishers first, and if none of them were interested, she'd make inquiries about getting the novels printed privately. She even had a list prepared of the order in which she wanted them re-issued. But there was something about her manner which annoyed Clive. She seemed to take it for granted that he'd meet the expense without any argument. He said she kept using the word 'we' although at no point in the conversation did she ask for his opinion. As far as she was concerned, it was all cut and dried. He said he suddenly felt *used* by her. Used. That was his word for it. He realised for the first time that William's attitude to him had been exactly the same. It had never been a real relationship, his and William's, any more than his with Imogen. Both of them, in their different ways, had sucked him dry. Realising this, he said he didn't want to appear to give in to her too easily, even if he put up only a token protest. But he hadn't bargained for her reaction. He blames himself for that. He said he should have known that she'd take it badly. She saw it, of course, as another form of betrayal and so she threatened him."

"With what?" Rudd asked.

"With publishing a biography of her brother in which Clive's love affair with William would have been exposed."

"So that was it," Rudd said quietly. He had suspected that it would be something of that sort, although he hadn't guessed its exact nature. He had already concluded that Imogen Kershaw had some hold over Osborne, some secret from his past, evidence for which Osborne feared had been contained in those files of memorabilia in the manuscript room and which he had searched through hurriedly, looking presumably for any evidence of his affair with Kershaw. In his haste, he had neglected to put them back in the right order, rousing not only Rudd's suspicions but Scott's as well.

"Would she have carried out her threat?" he asked.

Scott roused himself into a semblance of animation, his hands jerking upwards in utter repudiation of the idea.

"Of course not! And if Clive hadn't been so distressed by the situation, he would have realised that himself. But he was too angry to think rationally. All he could see was that Imogen intended to destroy what little he had left—his reputation and social standing in the town—if she went ahead. But Imogen had no intention of doing anything of the sort. It would have ruined William's reputation, at least in her eyes, as much as Clive's. It was the last thing she wanted to admit about her brother—that he was a homosexual. It was at this point that I tried ringing her for the second time. As I'd thought, she hadn't bothered to answer the phone when I rang before at half past eight because she'd been busy upstairs sorting through William's papers.

"It was unfortunate timing on my part but how was I to know that she and Clive were in the middle of a quarrel? They were both standing up near the fireplace, facing one another. Imogen had to go past Clive to get to the phone and he wouldn't move out of the way. He wanted, he said, to have the whole business out in the open and he felt she was using the fact that the phone was ringing and she had to answer it as an excuse to avoid the issue. She pushed past him quite angrily, lost her balance and fell, striking her head against the fender.

"Clive said it was like a nightmare. He picked her up and tried to revive her but he couldn't find a pulse. He thought she was dead and he'd be blamed for it. And all the time the bloody phone went on ringing. He went into the hall to take the receiver off. He'd intended calling an ambulance when he'd done that but, as he got to it, the phone suddenly stopped. He said the silence was even worse than the sound of its ringing. He couldn't remember exactly what he was thinking at the time, except for an overwhelming feeling of panic and rage which seemed to burst inside his head. There's that brass container full of William's walking-sticks next to the table where the phone is. He must have picked one up before going back into the sitting-room although he couldn't recall doing either. When he came to, so to speak, he found himself standing over her and hitting her with the stick and the blood was running down her face."

Scott covered his own face with his hands, turning away so that the Chief Inspector could not see his tears.

Rudd said, "I think that's enough, Mr. Scott. I'm going to ask you to stop there. You can tell me the rest some other time when you've recovered a little from the shock."

Not that he really needed Scott to complete the account for him, although he'd have to take a full statement from the man at some point in order that Osborne's confession could be officially recorded. The remainder he could guess. After Imogen Kershaw's murder, Osborne had wiped his prints from the walking-stick, putting on Kershaw's gloves while he faked the burglary and using the pocket-knife from one of the display cabinets to prise open the lock on the French doors. But, knowing that the desk and chair stood just inside the windows, he had been too careful about creating this part of the supposed break-in. Instead of forcing the doors violently open as any real burglar would have done, unaware that the furniture stood in the way, Osborne had levered them inwards gently to avoid breaking the glass, afraid perhaps that the noise might arouse the neighbours.

After that, Rudd assumed, Osborne had checked that there was nothing in the manuscript room among Kershaw's private papers which referred to his homosexual relationship with Kershaw, and then had left the house through the French windows, taking with him a few items of value to give credence to the apparent motive of theft and hiding the gloves in the bushes before escaping into the alleyway, but forgetting in his haste to bolt the front door.

It would have taken him about a quarter of an hour to walk by the back streets to the station, in time for the arrival of the London train at 10:35.

Rudd got to his feet and stood for a few moments looking down at Scott.

The man was sitting sideways in his chair, twisted awkwardly away from him, his face still hidden in his hands.

Rudd said, "I'd like you to get ready to leave, Mr. Scott. I've sent for a doctor. He should be here any minute now."

He arrived as Rudd was helping Scott on with his overcoat, which the Chief Inspector had retrieved from a chair in the hall under his own duffel.

Scott stood obediently to allow Rudd to drape it over his shoulders, rather as an exhausted child might submit to the ministrations of an adult, before being led away by the doctor who, in a whispered consultation with the Chief Inspector, expressed the opinion that Scott should be admitted to hospital for observation.

"They'll sedate him," he added. "In a couple of days he should be over the worst of it."

On the doorstep, Scott paused and turned back as if struck by a sudden thought.

"If you're wondering where the things are from the museum, you'll find them upstairs in Clive's bedroom. He had his briefcase with him and he put them all into that, including the Palmer drawing, to make it look as if there'd been a burglary."

Rudd couldn't resist asking, "Why did he take that?"

Scott stood quite still, head on one side, as he considered the question.

Then he said, "Because it was beautiful and William had always loved it. That was the only reason. Clive wanted it to remind him of the time when they had both been happy."

The next moment, he had gone, shambling out of the house, the doctor shepherding him down the steps, and the door closed behind him.

CHAPTER SIXTEEN

Even then the events of the night weren't over, although by the time Boyce arrived, day was breaking.

Rudd, extinguishing the lamps in the drawing-room and pulling back the curtains, revealed a sky which was growing pallid with the first few reddish streaks of dawn. In its vaporous light, the garden and its surrounding trees looked colourless, drenched in grey moisture, the foliage heavy and motionless.

He and the Sergeant sat on either side of the fire which had sunk back on itself, the tinder shifting and creaking as the logs subsided into the ash, while they waited for the WPC to arrive to take over the vigil on behalf of Mrs. Wharton, Clive Osborne's housekeeper, who was still asleep, thank God, upstairs. The last thing Rudd wanted to cope with was a middle-aged woman in a state of distress.

There had been no positive news from Bayliss at the incident room. Osborne's BMW had not been sighted. It could be hours, perhaps days, before it was found.

Rudd had padded out to the kitchen to make tea for himself and Boyce, rummaging as silently as he could in unfamiliar cupboards, looking for sugar and cups and listening, as he waited for the kettle to boil, to the dawn chorus as the birds in Osborne's garden stirred into life and lifted their voices with the growing light. It sounded sweetly poignant.

They drank the tea round the remains of the fire, talking in low voices as Rudd briefed the Sergeant on the night's events, including the arrest of Lucy Blake and Jed Kemp.

Boyce said, "What the hell put you on to Osborne in the first place?"

"His overcoat. Remember when we talked to his housekeeper she said after he came home on Wednesday and rang Scott, she took his coat upstairs to hang it up to dry? It didn't mean much at the time. It was only when I saw Kemp being taken off for questioning that I made the connection. He was wearing one of those shiny waterproof jackets and, under the lights, it looked wet through. I checked later with Fowles, the man who'd been on the beat on the night of the murder and who'd seen Scott coming away from the museum. He told me it'd started raining quite heavily that evening at twenty past ten although it'd only lasted for about ten minutes. But at that time Osborne, according to his alibi, should've been on the train from London, the one that left Liverpool Street at 9:25. So how and when had Osborne's coat got wet? Not in London. He told us he'd missed the earlier train by a few minutes and waited on the station for the next. But Liverpool Street's under cover. I remembered waiting there myself yesterday evening to catch a train home and noticing the roof. There was no way he could've got caught in the rain there. It made me question his whole alibi."

"Then how the hell did he fake it?" Boyce demanded. "Kyle checked with the ticket collector at Selhaven. The man knew Osborne by sight and was quite positive he'd come off the later train. He remembered him handing in his ticket."

"Chadwick put me on to that one although I didn't pay much attention either to what he said. It was when we were checking on the time he left Selhaven on Wednesday afternoon. He said he couldn't prove he'd caught the 5:12 train. There was no-one on the barrier when he went on to the platform. I had a chat with a porter earlier this morning after I'd spoken with Fowles. Selhaven's a small station and, because of manning levels, there often isn't a ticket-collector on duty for arrivals unless there happens to be a train departing at about the same time. It isn't necessary. There's an inspector on the trains checking tickets anyway. The 8:10 from London is one of those. So with no train due to depart, Osborne was able to walk off the station without handing in his ticket. He must have slipped it into his pocket without thinking. I don't believe he intended then to use it to set up an alibi. But it must have already crossed his mind that Imogen Kershaw's plan to re-issue her brother's books was going to involve him. There was no chance any publisher would be interested. Scott made that quite clear the first time we interviewed him. They'd have to be privately printed and Osborne would be expected to foot the bill as he'd done in the past. We'll probably only find out to what extent when we check his accounts."

"So it was blackmail?" Boyce asked.

"In a way, yes. Guilt money is probably a better term for it. I don't think Imogen Kershaw went about it quite as blatantly as a professional blackmailer. It was much more subtle than that. I imagine all she did was ask Osborne's advice about bills she had to meet. How was she going to manage to pay the rates, the electricity, the repairs? And, because he felt he owed her something for William Kershaw's sake as well as hers, Osborne forked out. But settling a few household bills was one thing. Being expected to finance the cost of republishing Kershaw's novels was another. According to Scott, Osborne brooded about it all the time he was in London, and when he got off the train at Selhaven, he decided to walk round to the museum and talk it over with her in more detail."

Rudd, who had already given Boyce a brief resumé of Scott's statement, added, "We know what happened next. They quarrelled, she fell and hit her head against the fender and Osborne, not only angry but panic-stricken, struck her several times with the walking-stick. It was then a quarter to ten. We can fix the time from Scott's phone call. In fact, it was the sound of the phone ringing which set off the whole sequence of events." He gave Boyce a wry smile. "Bloody ironic, isn't it? Scott calls Imogen Kershaw because he's worried about her and, in effect, triggers off her murder.

"We know what happened after that. In fact, we can time Osborne's movements fairly accurately. He had to fake the burglary and that's why, incidentally, that first display cabinet was smashed open. Osborne wanted to get to the penknife to prise open the other cabinet and force the lock on the French windows. He then had to check the files in the manuscript room to make sure there was nothing in Kershaw's papers about their affair, and clear out of the house in time to put in an appearance when the 10:35 arrived from London. He didn't have long and that's why he made mistakes, like putting the files back in the wrong order and forgetting to bolt the front door. And there was one thing he hadn't bargained for—the rain. It must have started when he was walking back to the station through the side streets. It probably didn't even cross his mind that it was significant. Once he got to the station, it was a simple matter for him to climb over the fence from the car-park as the train drew in, walk up the platform with the other passengers and hand in his ticket. It seemed foolproof. Mrs. Wharton could confirm his alibi. He arrived home at quarter to eleven, ten minutes after the train, the time it'd take him to walk from the station. There was no way, it seemed, that he could have had the opportunity to murder Imogen Kershaw and if it hadn't been for that overcoat of his, he'd've got away with it."

"He was home but not dry," Boyce said, pulling a face at his own pun. "By the way," he went on, "Kyle reported in after I got back from London. He checked up on Lucy Blake at London University like you asked him. She was there all right but got chucked out for—guess what?"

"Smoking pot?" Rudd suggested.

He felt too exhausted to play verbal games with the Sergeant.

"How did you know that? Oh, I get it. We smelt the stuff when we went round to interview her."

"Partly," Rudd admitted. "But I guessed she hadn't had a nervous breakdown. She was too hard a bitch for that. She was simply stringing Miss Kershaw along. She's got a lot to answer for, has that young woman."

He didn't bother to add that he held Lucy Blake largely responsible for putting the idea into Imogen Kershaw's head of having her brother's books republished. But you couldn't charge anybody with malice. He could only hope that, when she came up for trial on the drug-smuggling charge, they'd throw the bloody book at her.

Boyce went on discussing the case, moving on to Chadwick and how the missing Palmer had turned out to be a false lead after all, just as the Sergeant had suspected. Although he didn't say it outright, his remarks implied as much; a small piece of self-vindication which Rudd didn't begrudge him. He was relieved though when the front doorbell rang, announcing the arrival of the WPC, rousing him from his torpor and at the same time effectively shutting Boyce up.

They left soon afterwards, driving the short distance to Selhaven police station, Boyce at the wheel, Rudd slumped in the passenger seat, fighting off an overwhelming desire to put his head back and catch up on some sleep. Even five minutes' oblivion would have been welcome.

The town was already stirring, even though it was Sunday morning. The newsagent's opposite Dolcis shoe-shop was open and a porter had come out of the King's Head Hotel to water the tubs of hydrangeas on either side of the swing doors, and to sweep away the dead leaves which had accumulated overnight on the steps.

They waited in Bayliss's office for news of Osborne, Rudd drowsing and Boyce occasionally breaking in to start up a desultory conversation, made uncomfortable by too long a silence.

"I forgot to mention it before," he remarked at one point, "but while Kyle was checking up on Lucy Blake in London, he discovered a bit about her background. She's the daughter of some important surgeon—top bloke at one of the London hospitals. Makes you think, doesn't it?"

"Yes," Rudd said, opening one eye and immediately shutting it again. He was used to answering automatically when Boyce was in this chatty mood.

It was ten o'clock before the call came. A Sergeant brought the information from the incident room. A car had been seen in the river at Tolstead by someone out in a dinghy—the same village, as Rudd pointed out to Boyce on the way there, where Kershaw had rented a cottage during the war when he had been working on a farm and where, according to Scott, Osborne had stayed during his army leaves. He didn't add that the place probably held memories for Osborne of happier days, before the relationship with Kershaw had turned sour.

The place was insignificant; a few farm cottages, one of which was probably where Kershaw and his sister had lived—there was no way of telling; a bus-stop; a tin chapel; not even a church.

They turned down a lane, similar to the one, Rudd imagined, that he had taken in the dark on his own route to the river to meet up with the police launch—when was it? Only a few hours ago. It seemed a lifetime away. There was a similar rutted track, and a vista of flat fields and wide sky, and the same river odour coming in through the car windows.

At the end of it, they found a small wooden landing-stage, composed of planks and piles, jutting out, because it was low tide, into the mud, its boards echoing with a familiar hollow sound as Rudd, getting out of the car, walked on to it.

Osborne's BMW lay several feet beyond its edge, embedded on its side in the ooze, its windows open. So he had meant to kill himself, Rudd thought. Osborne's death couldn't be written off as an accident. And no doubt Scott had known, when Osborne had driven off in the car, what had been his intention. No wonder Scott had looked so relieved when Rudd had turned up at the house.

Boyce was saying, "Christ, what a waste!" but whether he meant Osborne's death or the condition of the car, he didn't specify and Rudd, giving him the benefit of the doubt, took the remark to refer to both. "Must have gone in at high tide," the Sergeant added. "It's going to be a hell of a job to get it out."

He made the last comment with a certain satisfaction. After all, it wasn't his problem.

Rudd went on contemplating the car in silence. There was no sign of Osborne inside it, thank God. That particular horror would come later. And there was no point in hanging about waiting for the recovery vehicle to turn up. Bayliss, who had accompanied them in his own car, could be left in charge of that.

As he turned away, he heard faintly in the distance the sound of church bells, carried on the wind from some unseen tower or steeple, summoning the congregation to morning prayer. It seemed a fitting note on which to leave.

Returning to Osborne's house later with a search warrant, they found Mrs. Wharton out of bed and tearful at finding Osborne gone and the WPC in charge. Rudd delegated the job of breaking the news to Mrs. Wharton of Osborne's death to the WPC, leaving the two of them shut up in the drawing-room as he and Boyce, together with Wylie—summoned from the golf-course and not too pleased at having to forfeit his Sunday game —went up the stairs to Osborne's bedroom.

He had evidently moved out of the matrimonial double bed and into a smaller single room overlooking the back garden—a change prompted perhaps by the death of his wife and the memories of their unhappy marriage.

There was no need to search far for the items missing from the museum. They lay in the bottom of the chest of drawers, wrapped in paper and sealed with sticky tape. Rudd put the parcel down on Osborne's bed to unwrap it, revealing the miscellany of objects, including Kershaw's penknife, which Osborne had snatched up after the murder, before standing back to watch as Wylie bagged them separately and entered them in the exhibits' register.

Only two items seemed to catch the Chief Inspector's attention and he bent down to examine them before they were packed away. One was a photograph in a silver frame which had stood, according to Scott, on Kershaw's desk and which, although Rudd wasn't aware of it, Nina had also taken particular notice of for much the same reason.

The faces of the three undergraduates in the punt gazed back at him, all young, all smiling with that confidence of youth which believes it has a whole lifetime of happiness in front of it.

And out of the three of them two were now dead, one of whom, God help him, Rudd had resented because he thought he'd had it too bloody easy. He jerked his head at Wylie to indicate that he could put the photograph away with the other objects. He'd finished with it.

He spent as long over the Palmer drawing which lay at the bottom of the parcel, wrapped up in its own sheet of paper. Looking at it, he could understand Nina's enthusiasm, even Chadwick's desire to own it. It was indeed beautiful; a small piece of English woodland captured on paper, redolent of summer and the scent of leaves.

He remembered glades like that from his boyhood; secret places under the trees, rustling with unseen creatures, the sun glancing in through the foliage and speckling the ground—soft with moss and leaf-litter—with flecks of green light which moved and seemed to breathe.

It occurred to him that this was probably why Osborne had taken it; not only because Kershaw had liked it, but because it had reminded Osborne of the far-off, innocent days of his own childhood, when friendship had meant nothing more than a companion with whom one shared those long, hot sunlit days under the high, blue skies of summer.

They left soon afterwards, conferring briefly in the hall with the WPC, who had arranged for Mrs. Wharton to stay with a sister in Chelmsford.

It was almost six o'clock when Rudd returned home, letting himself into the hall and stripping off the duffel coat which he flung down over the end of the bannisters before going upstairs to bath and change.

Coming down again afterwards, he found there was nothing to eat except a boil-in-the-bag beef stew which he took from the freezer, the stocks of which were running low. Once he became involved in a case, routine household chores like shopping tended to go by the board.

Dropping it into a pan of boiling water, he watched it bubble for a few moments and then, on an impulse, left it to simmer and went into the hall.

When the phone rang, Nina was washing her hair, kneeling by the side of the bath, her head under the shower. At first, she didn't hear it through the noise of the running water, but when at last she became aware of its ringing, she grabbed up a towel and ran to answer it, thinking it was Danny, phoning her at last. He hadn't been in touch with her since her return from Selhaven, and, on the occasions when she'd tried his number, there had been no reply.

Snatching up the receiver in mid-peal, she said breathlessly, "Yes?"

The voice at the other end of the line wasn't Danny's, although it sounded familiar.

"Nina?" it said. "It's Jack Rudd."

Like a fool, she could think of nothing else to say in her surprise except to repeat the word "Yes?"

"Have I rung at an awkward time?" he asked. He sounded a little on the defensive as if, having screwed up his courage to ring her, he was disappointed by her lack of response.

"No, no!" she answered quickly, anxious to put him right. "It's just that I was washing my hair and I'm wet and dripping all over the carpet. But it's all right." She suddenly began to laugh. "It's nice to hear from you."

He said, his voice warmer but still with that defensive note in it, as if he were prepared to be turned down, "I wondered if we could meet for dinner one evening this week? That is, if you're free."

Free! She had no-one else to think about except Danny. And sod him. If he turned up, he could cook his own meal for once.

She guessed, too, that Rudd was used to being rebuffed by that woman he'd told her about—Marion someone or other. Making her own voice sound warm and eager, she said, "I'd love to. What about Friday?"

"Fine. I'll pick you up at the flat at seven, shall I?" he suggested and rang off.

Nina put down her own receiver and returned to the bathroom where she finished rinsing her hair, thinking, as the water
showered over her head, "I'll book in for a proper shampoo and
set on Friday morning. And, God, what shall I wear!"

As for Rudd, he stood for a few moments in the hall, also
considering.

He had made the call on the spur of the moment, but he was
committed now. He could hardly ring back and cancel the ar-
rangement.

And why the hell should he?